IRON
THUNDER

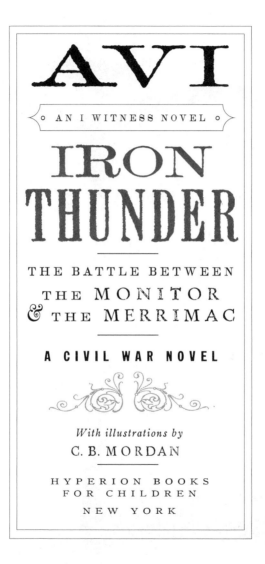

AVI

AN I WITNESS NOVEL

IRON THUNDER

THE BATTLE BETWEEN
THE MONITOR
& THE MERRIMAC

A CIVIL WAR NOVEL

With illustrations by
C. B. MORDAN

HYPERION BOOKS
FOR CHILDREN
NEW YORK

For Jeff Oliver
From Brooklyn to Virginia
—

CONTENTS

CHAPTER ONE
How It Began · 3

CHAPTER TWO
I Get a Job on I Don't Know What · 7

CHAPTER THREE
I Meet a Genius · 14

CHAPTER FOUR
I Gaze Upon Something Strange · 20

CHAPTER FIVE
I See Gold in the Snow · 24

CHAPTER SIX
I Don't Tell the Truth · 28

CHAPTER SEVEN
I Learn Some Big Things · 33

CHAPTER EIGHT
I Meet Mr. Ogden Quinn · 40

CHAPTER NINE
I Learn the Ship's Name · 47

CHAPTER TEN
I Battle for the *Monitor* · 52

CHAPTER ELEVEN
I Have a Meeting · 57

CHAPTER TWELVE
I Go to Garrett Falloy · 63

CHAPTER THIRTEEN
I Ride the *Monitor* Into the East River · 68

CHAPTER FOURTEEN
I Escape · 75

CHAPTER FIFTEEN
I Find a Place of Safety · 78

CHAPTER SIXTEEN
I Get a Surprise · 86

CHAPTER SEVENTEEN
My Life Inside the *Monitor* · 97

CHAPTER EIGHTEEN
We're Almost Ready · 104

CHAPTER NINETEEN
We Make Our Final Preparations · 110

CHAPTER TWENTY
The Night Before Departure · 116

CHAPTER TWENTY-ONE

I Say Farewell to Brooklyn · 127

CHAPTER TWENTY-TWO

Disaster! · 134

CHAPTER TWENTY-THREE

Desperate · 139

CHAPTER TWENTY-FOUR

We Arrive at Hampton Roads · 144

CHAPTER TWENTY-FIVE

The Pilot's News · 150

CHAPTER TWENTY-SIX

I See a Sight I Never Wish to See Again · 156

CHAPTER TWENTY-SEVEN

The Morning of March 9, 1862 · 162

CHAPTER TWENTY-EIGHT

The Battle Starts · 167

CHAPTER TWENTY-NINE

The Battle Continues · 179

CHAPTER THIRTY

Who Won? · 188

GLOSSARY

193

AUTHOR'S NOTE

199

THE MONITOR TODAY

201

BIBLIOGRAPHY

203

April 13, 1861

THE NEW YORK HERALD

The War Begun!

Very Exciting News from Charleston

Bombardment of Fort Sumter Commenced

The Summons to Major Anderson to SURRENDER

MAJOR ANDERSON'S REFUSAL

Terrible Fire from the Secessionist Batteries

Ma and I had halted at the dim bottom steps of the shabby York Street tenement . . .

CHAPTER ONE

How It Began

"Tom, we just need more money. You're going to have to take your pa's place."

It was a cold early evening in January 1862, and the war had been going ten months. But only a week had passed since we'd learned that my pa had been killed fighting in some town in Maryland. We didn't know where exactly. No more than we knew if his remains would be returned. The only thing we did know was that he was gone—forever.

Ma and I had halted at the dim bottom steps of the shabby York Street tenement, where we lived in the Vinegar Hill section of Brooklyn. I'd been carrying home one of her laundry loads. So when she sent my older sister, Dora, on up ahead, telling her to light the wood stove, I thought she just wanted to take a rest. The three flights up to our rooms always tired her.

Her words gave me two feelings: some kind of pride she'd consider me able, but upset that she'd ask me to take over from Pa. I didn't see how I could. His dying left me sad, and angry too, at the army, at the Union, at President Lincoln for taking my pa away and altering our lives in ways I could not know. Getting a job was the first big change.

Like lots of boys, I'd been peddling newspapers—the *Herald*—around the neighborhood. You could pull in buyers if you called out the war headlines right. I may have been small for my thirteen years, but I was loud. Thing is, since I had to buy the papers before I sold them, I made, maybe, thirty-five cents a week. The best corner was right outside the Brooklyn Navy Yard gates. But Garrett Falloy, being the biggest newsboy around, had that one.

I was going to the local school. Well, some days, at least. Liked it fair enough. Learned to read, anyway.

"What kind of work you figure I could get?" I said, adding, "And I won't join no army."

She looked at me so mournful I wished I hadn't spoken. "Tom," she whispered, "you know I wouldn't want that."

We all knew what was happening with the rebellion. About ten months ago—when Mr. Lincoln became president—eleven southern states left the Union. Claimed they were an independent country. Named themselves the Confederate States of America. Rebels or "secesh" is what we called them. Back in April, they began the war by firing on Fort Sumter down in South Carolina.

When the war began, lots of neighborhood men and boys signed up for Brooklyn's Fourteenth Regiment. My father did. Maybe they believed in the Union, like my pa. I supposed it was the pay, too. We needed money, and a private made thirteen dollars a month.

The truth is, no one thought the war was going to last so long or be so bloody. But by early winter, though newspapers said otherwise, folks knew the war wasn't going well. Not for the Union. Lots, like my pa, had been killed.

We got along because Ma and my sister each earned about two dollars a week by taking in officers' washing from the nearby Navy Yard. But my sister made less because she got sick a lot. So I knew my ma was right. We needed more money.

"What do you think I could do?" I asked.

"I spoke to the yardmaster today," she said. "Mr. Hendricks. He might need help."

"Doing what?"

"Not sure," she said. "Said I should just bring you around tomorrow."

Trudging upstairs that night, I had no idea what would happen. I felt like an ox must when a yoke is thrown over its neck for the first time. I supposed school was over. But if you'd told me then I was going to be part of the most amazing adventure of the whole war, I'd have called you a liar—flat out.

Except it was no lie—I was there—I saw it all.

CHAPTER TWO

I Get a Job on I Don't Know What

I T WAS STILL DARK next morning when I heard, "Tom! Get up!" My sister, Dora, was standing over me with a cup of coffee in one hand, lit candle in another. "Ma's almost ready," she whispered.

Dora was seventeen and worried about me a lot. No more than I worried about her. Thin and pale, she coughed too much. And it was so cold that January, the East River was clogged with ice. Mostly she stayed home.

I got up, threw cold water on my face, hot coffee into my belly. As we left, Dora slipped a piece of bread and molasses into my hand.

Ma led the way to the Brooklyn Navy Yard. Those days, Brooklyn was the country's third biggest city, right behind New York and Philadelphia. But the Yard,

This is the entrance to the Brooklyn Navy Yard.
Usually it was very cluttered and busy.

perched on the East River opposite New York City, was a city itself. There were many huge warehouses and open workshops where cord was twined and canvas sails stitched. Cranes for lifting heavy things. Coils of rope lay everywhere. Mounds of cannonballs were set in pyramid fashion, the cannons lined up in rows like so many giant iron bottles ready to pour out fire and hot shot. The air, cold though it was, smelled of hot tar, cut wood, and brackish sea.

People said the Yard had never been so busy. That was because when the war began, Mr. Lincoln told the

Union navy to close down the Southern ports—a block-ade. Called it the "Anaconda Plan," after that huge snake that kills by squeezing. It's what the Union wanted to do to the Rebels—choke the fighting out of them. But to do it, the Union needed ships. That's why the dry docks were full of ships—sail and paddle—being refit or new-made. Mechanics, laborers, sailors, and sol-diers, almost all men, but some boys, were working day and night.

Guards with rifles were on tight watch at the gates. Secessionist spies and saboteurs—I'm not say-ing just Southerners either—were said to be everywhere. "Copper-heads," is what we called those traitors.

Ma led me to the Yard's central court, to the Round House. It was a big, four-story building, not really round but eight-sided with a great clock set in one wall so people could mark time. It's

The Round House.
The big clock is on the far side.

where workers signed up and pay was passed out.

We slipped through the crowds to a door that was split in two, with the top half opening outward, the bottom half fitted with a shelf. Over the door was a sign:

MR. HENDRICKS
YARDMASTER

Ma knocked on the shelf. "Mr. Hendricks, sir!" she called.

An old gent with a curly gray beard appeared. He was wearing a blue navy uniform.

"Ah, Mrs. Carroll, ma'am," said this Hendricks with a tip of his navy cap. "Morning!"

"Mr. Hendricks, sir," said my mother, nudging me forward, "I told you I'd be bringing my son. Name's Thomas Carroll, though most everybody calls him Tom."

"Do they, now?" said Mr. Hendricks, fixing his eyes like he was measuring me for a Sunday suit. I don't doubt he saw what there was: a kid with brown hair crowning a face with dark eyes, thick eyebrows, and ears to grow into, but no more blarney than most. As usual, I was wearing a checked flannel shirt, baggy trousers held up by braces, plus boots and a cloth cap.

"What kind of work would that be, now?" he asked me.

"Most anything that's fitting, sir," I muttered. "I'm more than willing."

"You don't look particular willing," he said, laughing. "How old?"

"Thirteen," I said.

"Small for your age, ain't you?" said Mr. Hendricks.

"He's very strong," said Ma, bringing heat to my face.

Mr. Hendricks nodded. "And I suppose he'll take anything that's offered?"

"Yes, sir," Ma said quickly. "We're in sore need."

"You and everybody else," Hendricks muttered. All the same, he gave me another sharp look as if to pin me in place, then picked up a ledger book.

"A boy your size . . ." he muttered to himself, turning pages. "Here's the ticket," he said, jabbing a finger down. "Rowland's Continental Iron Works. Greenpoint. About a mile or so upriver."

"What's there?" asked Ma.

Mr. Hendricks grinned. "They're bolting Ericsson's floating battery together. Need all the help they can get."

"What's a floating battery?" I asked.

"Something new in navy ways," said the yard-master. "An ironclad ship." He added a wink and said,

"Useful, I suppose, *if* she floats." He pushed *if* more than he did *useful*.

"What's her name?" I asked, thinking a ship with a brave name would be worth working on. A good brag, anyway.

Mr. Hendricks laughed. "No real name yet. But folks are calling her 'Ericsson's Folly.' They say she'll have tight quarters, so you could be a help."

I thought of a smart answer to his mocking words, but kept my mouth shut.

"Now then," he said, "for a likely boy, they'll pay a whole seventy-five cents a week."

I was sure we needed more, but when I glanced at Ma she nodded.

"I'll take it," I said without much enthusiasm.

"Yours, then," said Mr. Hendricks. He wrote out an order on a yellow chit of paper and handed it down. "With my compliments. Just give this to Mr. Ericsson," he said.

"Who's he?" I asked.

"The man building that floating pot," he said. Then he added, "But I suppose the Union needs pots, too, right?"

I thought, but didn't say, Don't care beans for pots or the Union.

Not talking, Ma and I went back out through the

Yard gates. Lacy snow was floating down.

When we reached the horse trolley stop, she offered me a penny for the ride, saying, "Do you know where Rowland's Iron Works is?"

I nodded, saying, "I can walk."

"Tom, don't be angry. We need the money."

"Not you I'm angry at," I said, fighting back tears and keeping my face down.

"Who, then?"

"Doesn't matter."

She sighed. "You warm enough?"

"Fine."

She touched my face. "Now, Tom," she whispered, "honor to your father's name."

"I don't see any honor in making pots."

She stood still a moment—eyes looking I don't know where—but then said, "Tom, best get on. I've got to collect my washing."

I started off. After a few steps I turned. "Ma! What's an . . . *ironclad?*"

"Don't know," she said.

I watched her walk back slowly through the snow toward the Yard. If I could have thought of something to say, I would've. Instead, hands in my pockets, I headed for the ironworks. All I could think was, Don't care beans for pots or the Union.

CHAPTER THREE

I Meet a Genius

WHEN I GOT to the gates of the ironworks there was a military guard talking to a blue-frock-coated policeman. I offered my yellow slip to the guard. He glanced at it, handed it back. "Mr. Ericsson, eh?" he said, winking like it was some joke.

"Working on his iron coffin, are you?" the policeman chimed in.

I thought of flinging back something like *It'll fit you fine!*, but, not wanting to sass a policeman, I held back.

"You'll find the genius in his shack down by the river," said the guard, waving me through. "Straight on. Can't miss it. 'Less you want to!"

I hesitated. "Why would I?"

"You know what people say: not much difference 'tween a genius and a madman!"

Lord, I'd barely heard of this Ericsson but he was being tarred with scorn: *Floating pot! Iron coffin! Madman!* It made me nervous. But I admit, I was curious, too. *What* was the man making?

When I got to the wooden shack I'd been directed to, I found the door left ajar. I peeked in. A man was bent over a table, pencil in hand, the table layered over with large sheets of paper marked up with a whirl of lines.

I knocked on the door frame. The man didn't answer. Knocked again, louder. That time the man turned, and I got my first look at John Ericsson.

He was a stocky fellow with wide shoulders and a great dome of a forehead. Sideburns came down to his chin, which made it look like his jaw stuck out, as if he were daring you to punch it. He had a strong, almost scowling mouth. I thought, The man's a prizefighter.

John Ericsson really liked this picture of himself because it made him appear big and strong.

"Yes?" he asked, not bothering to hide his annoyance.

"Looking for Mr. Ericsson, sir."

"*Captain* Ericsson," he said.

My thought was, Oh-oh. A corrector. "Begging pardon, sir. *Captain* Ericsson."

"All right, then. What do you want?" He had a slight foreign accent.

I held out my paper. "Reporting for work, sir," I said. "On your . . . your . . . don't know what you call her, sir."

"My floating battery?"

"Yes, sir," I said, trying to be respectful. "I suppose so."

"Do you know what she is?"

"No, sir. Don't."

He considered me again, took the paper, scanned it, and tossed it on his table. "Then what work do you intend to do?"

"Sir," I blurted out in frustration, "or Captain, or Mister, all I know is I was sent here from the Brooklyn Navy Yard. Mr. Hendricks sends his compliments. Said you'd pay seventy-five cents a week to a small boy."

"Why small?"

"Because you're making something small enough for me to fit into."

He let slip a hint of a smile. "On that account

alone," he said, "you'll qualify. Be with you soon." He turned back to marking his drawings.

There was a potbellied stove in the corner, but it wasn't being used. All I could do was rub my hands and stamp my feet against the chill. Feeling stupid and cold, I didn't have much choice but to sit on the floor just inside his door and wait. Still, waiting there, I had plenty of time to take in the ironworks.

It was a lot smaller than the Brooklyn Navy Yard, with none of the Yard's wood and tar smells or tapping hammers. Instead, lots of black smoke, roaring sounds, and the stink of I knew not what, though it did make my eyes, nose, and ears itch. There were machines making awful clanking noises. Near as I could tell, iron ingots were being shaped and cut. Lots of thick-armed blacksmiths, too, pounding more iron.

And there were great furnaces glowing fiery red heat, reminding me of that place boys had to work hard to avoid. In the Brooklyn Navy Yard, fire was the enemy. Here, fire was a tool. Made me think, This is no place for making ships.

I waited on Captain Ericsson at least an hour. All that time he didn't look around or say one word. I sat there wondering if there wasn't a better way to earn some money.

But finally the man left off his work. "Come with

me," he barked, as if only a moment had passed. Paper scroll in hand, top hat on his head, frock coat buttoned, he strode out of the shed.

"Name's Tom, is it?" he said as I tried to keep up. As I'd learn, John Ericsson never went anywhere slowly.

"Yes, sir."

"Can you read, write, do sums?"

"I've been attending school," I told him.

"Just attending?" He frowned, but left off the subject. "Do you know who I am?"

"Captain Ericsson, sir," I said, making sure I said *Captain*.

"Captain in the Swedish army. I've invented machines, motors, locomotives, ships, as well as the screw propeller for most ships."

I took another look up at him.

"Now then," he went on, "we're working on my latest invention. A ship. I have designed it to save the Union."

Wondering why he was saying these things to me, a boy, all I said was, "I'm sure you will, sir."

"Good. You'll take your orders from me," he went on, "and from those to whom *I* delegate authority." He stopped and faced me with a frown. "Spies are everywhere. You will tell *no one* what you see here. Is that understood?"

Nothing for me to say but "Yes, sir."

He marched on. "I'm a married man," he continued, "but my wife resides in England. With my boy. It's been a while since I've seen them. My knowledge of boys comes mostly from my own memory. When I was sixteen, I was a surveyor for the Swedish army and had command of six hundred men."

"I heard say you are a genius," I said, wondering if he'd hear my sarcasm.

He glanced at me, nodded, and said, "You'll do."

Then I thought about what the guard had said: how geniuses were like madmen. Except, there I was, under tow, so to speak, and couldn't rightly break off. And I kept reminding myself that maybe seventy-five cents wasn't gold, but it could buy bread.

CHAPTER FOUR

I Gaze Upon Something Strange

I FOLLOWED CAPTAIN ERICSSON into a huge, open-ended woodshed. "There's my ship!" he said, his voice full of pride.

The East River was crowded with ships. So, like most anyone living in Brooklyn, I'd seen plenty of them. But what Captain Ericsson was showing me was like no ship I'd ever seen.

The thing before me had no masts, spars, or rope, which is to say nothing from which to hang sails. Which was the bow or stern, I couldn't guess. Just rounded ends. I figured it to be a hundred and seventy feet long—the measure of a really tall telegraph pole. It was forty or so feet wide, maybe sixteen feet deep, with straight sides.

Ship? It was more like a *raft*—flat as one of my ma's

A Brooklyn Navy Yard building shed.
It is very much like the ones at the Continental Iron Works.

Sunday griddle cakes. What might make her sail, or what she was supposed to *do*, I couldn't fathom.

I did see some wood—ten-inch-square oak beams held in place by wood angles. I figured that was her hull. As we stood there, swarms of mechanics and laborers were covering those beams with pine planking. And over that planking, other men were quick to slap on what looked like double sheets of half-inch iron, bolting them tight with rivets and bolts.

I'd been to the Navy Yard tons of times, helping Ma with laundry. Saw ships aplenty being made. Hard work, sure, but work as calm as Sunday—men knowing what to do the way I suppose shipbuilders knew since it started drizzling on Noah.

But what I was seeing here were men shouting, pushing each other out of the way, all of them trying to do this, that, and another thing, all at the same time. A jumble!

Then Captain Ericsson said, "Well, boy, don't you think she's fine?"

As fine as salted rat spit! I thought. Only, I wasn't going to say that. Not on the first day of a new job, and that job needed. The best I could offer was, "They're working pretty fast."

"We've only got a hundred days to build her," he said.

"Why's that?" I asked.

"Because, at this very moment, in Virginia, they are building a sea monster."

I looked at him. Sure as shooting, he *was* mad. "A sea monster?"

He gave a solemn nod. "A monster to destroy the Union. But my ship shall stop her dead in the water."

"How she going to do that?"

"She's covered with iron."

"Will she . . . float?"

"Of course!"

I turned from this odd man to the odder-looking ship being built. My first thought was, I don't think so. My second thought was to recall the guard's mocking words, *iron coffin*. My third notion was, Thank the Lord I won't be sailing on her, or—to put it right—sinking with her!

CHAPTER FIVE

I See Gold in the Snow

THAT FIRST DAY, I spent my time mostly running errands for Captain Ericsson, learning where things were, who was in charge of this and that. By the end of the day, I knew he wanted things fast and he wanted them right.

By quitting time, it was dark, snow was drifting down, and I was worn out. As I left through the gates with the other workers, I saw Luke, one of my pals, selling newspapers. Envying him his freedom, I gave him a nod and started the long walk home.

I moved from one pool of gas lamplight to another, bright islands in the muddy slush. I was thinking about the captain's ship, trying to grasp what she was. Mostly, though, I was just glad to be going home.

Crossing a street, I chanced to look back. Half a

block behind, a man was coming along in my footsteps. I paid him no mind. But after another few blocks, I looked around. He was still there, only a little closer. I thought, He's following me.

I walked faster, but it wasn't too long before I heard, "Hey, boy! Wait!"

I stopped but kept myself ready to bolt. When he was about twenty feet from me, I spun around and called, "What do you want? Why are you following me?"

The man halted in the darkness. All I could make out was that he was a thin fella, with a long coat and shiny boots. A slouch hat slipped a shadow over most of his face.

"You're working at the ironworks, aren't you?"

"What about it?"

"See anything of Ericsson's floating battery?"

That took me by surprise. "Maybe."

"I'd sure be interested in what you saw."

I said, "How come?"

"Just curious. Everybody's talking about it. What's your name?"

"Tom."

"Say, Tom, if you kept your eyes open and told me what you saw, you could make real money." All of a sudden, he pitched a coin at me that landed by my feet. I looked down. In the gaslight I could see a gold dollar glowing in the snow!

The man halted in the darkness.

"Go on," he said, laughing. "Pick it up. It's yours. More to come if you want it."

I looked at him and then at the coin. More than a week's pay right there! Truth is, I didn't think twice before I snatched it up and then took off fast as I could for our rooms.

Behind me, I could hear him calling, "You're with me now, Tom!"

As I galloped home, coin clutched in my hand, I kept thinking of Captain Ericsson's words: *You will tell no one what you see here. Spies are everywhere. Is that all understood?*

And I thought, That man's a Rebel spy! A copperhead! He wants me to spy!

I stopped short and looked at the coin. Though it gleamed pretty, I almost threw it away as something dirty, thinking, Copperhead coin. Then I had two more thoughts: Pa is gone. We need it. I didn't do anything. He just gave it to me. It's ours.

CHAPTER SIX

I Don't Tell the Truth

GOLD COIN DEEP in my pocket, I climbed to our place.

We lived in two rooms. The front one—our kitchen—had a wood stove and just one window, cracked. I hauled up water and wood. The other room had a bed, which my ma had shared with my father. My sister slept with her now. I had a cot at the foot. Our privy was in the backyard.

When I got there, Ma was working in the kitchen by the light of our hurricane lamp. She was folding a mound of sheets, shirts, and vests.

"How was it?" she asked, soon as I came through the door.

"Not sure," I said.

"What do you mean?"

"The man I'm working for is strange," I said. "A Swede. Some kind of inventor. Brags a lot."

"You'll stick with it, won't you?" she asked.

"Suppose," I said.

She set down a plate of cold boiled taters with a cut of bacon fry. I pitched in since I'd eaten nothing all day. She stood across from me, arms folded over her chest. The way she had with my father. It made me feel strange.

. . . Ma was working in the kitchen by the light of our hurricane lamp.

"You'll make some money," she said.

"Seventy-five cents."

"That's something."

Thinking about that gold dollar in my pocket, I wanted to give it to her, but didn't because I'd have to explain where I got it, and I didn't feel right about it.

"Where's Dora?" I asked.

"In bed. Feeling poorly."

When I finished eating, I went to our other room. Dora was sitting up in bed, Ma's coat around her. She was holding a handkerchief that was spotted with blood. A burning candle cast shadows on the walls.

I sat on the bed. Dora looked at me with her large, tired eyes. "Did you do well?" she asked, speaking soft like always. Being home so much, she was always asking about my outside doings.

"Good enough," I said. "Only, they're building something strange. A ship, they say. Except it sure don't look like one to me."

"Why, what's it look like?"

"Flat as the bottom of my shoe. And mostly iron."

"Iron! That's peculiar."

On impulse I held out the gold coin.

She looked at it, then at me. "That gold?"

"I found it on our street," I lied.

"Lucky! Did you tell Ma?"

I shook my head. "I don't think we should 'til we make sure no one claims it. Can you keep it safe for me?"

She wrapped the coin in her handkerchief.

"Tom," she said. "About your ship. Being iron, can it really float?"

"The man building her—Captain Ericsson—says so."

"Isn't that . . . foolish?"

"Seems so . . . but they pay me seventy-five cents, don't they?"

She smiled sadly. "Just don't sail on her."

January 18, 1862

THE PHILADELPHIA INQUIRER

GENERAL GRANT'S ARMY
NEAR COLUMBUS

News from
FORTRESS MONROE

Rebel Vessels
Captured in Gulf

The Town of Warrington
in Flames

CHAPTER SEVEN

I Learn Some Big Things

I'D TOLD DORA it was a strange ship they were building. That wasn't half. Ericsson bragged to me that she was like no ship *ever* built! Said he had some *forty* new inventions on her! Of course, that meant he was the only one who could give directions. Guess who carried each and every one? Me. I was more pack mule than boy.

I carried messages from this work crew to that. From Captain Ericsson—his spidery handwriting awful to read—to foremen, from foremen to Captain Ericsson. Questions asked, answered, asked again. Or I was fetching tea and coffee. The captain liked his tea strong and hot.

Most days—sometimes most hours—letters and telegraphs flew in from the Department of the Navy in

A letter from John Ericsson, written after the battle.
His writing was so light it seemed
he hardly touched his pen to the paper.

Washington. I carried them all—read them all. I learned *everything.*

I began to feel sorry for Captain Ericsson. The man was always working. Solving problems. Inventing what needed to be invented. Visiting all the places where parts were being made. Far as I could see, he didn't eat much, slept less. Short tempered? If he had a smile, it was still in Sweden!

Trying to keep up with him didn't give me much rest. By the time I'd get back home at night I was something tired. And when I got there, Dora had a million questions about what was happening at the Works.

"I don't fully understand," I admitted. "Every day we get telegraph messages from the Department of the Navy. They don't think the ship will work. Same time, they keep saying, 'Hurry up!'"

"Is it that hard to build?" she asked.

"I guess. All the iron parts are being made in different places. First we got to get them. Then they have to fit."

She laughed. "Like fixing a stew in a dozen kitchens all at once!"

"And another thing? Someone told me Captain Ericsson won't even get paid 'til it's done. He and some partners had to put up all the money."

"How much?"

"Two hundred and seventy-five thousand dollars!"

The best news was I hadn't seen that spy again. Which was fine because I wasn't sure what I'd say. One moment I'd think *gold dollars*. Next moment I'd think *copperhead*. And I have to admit, the more I worked at the ironworks, the more I fancied it. No two days were ever the same. No two hours, either!

I did get to know mechanics who were willing to answer my questions. I finally asked one—a lean, clean-shaven, strong-armed blacksmith by the name of Rory O'Keefe—*why* everything was being so rushed.

"Look here," he said, drawing a crude map with white chalk on a piece of rusty iron. "Here's the Atlantic coast. Here's us. Brooklyn. Down here, Virginia. Right here— the Elizabeth River. She flows right into Hampton Roads, on to the Chesapeake, on to the sea."

"What do you mean *roads*?" I asked.

"That's what they call a sheltered anchorage from the sea.

"At the head of the Chesapeake, the Potomac River and Washington, *our* capital. At the head of the James River sits Richmond. The Rebs' capital. Get it?"

I nodded.

"Now then, them secesh can't win their war alone. Need to trade with Europe. So we clamped a tight blockade at Hampton Roads, *here,* to lock them in. Okay. Lots of our ships are ready to fight—what they call *on station.* And our Fortress Monroe —biggest fort in the whole country—is nearby to help us. Long as we keep the Roads bottled up, them Rebels don't have a hair's chance on a bald man.

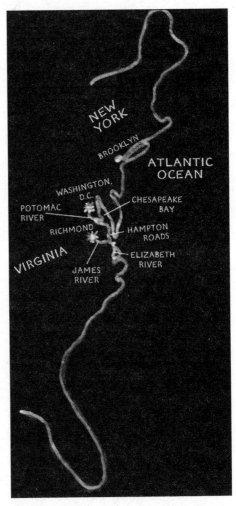

"Now, Mr. Lincoln says blockade everything from Chesapeake Bay to New Orleans. Easy to say. But when the war began, Tom, the Union had only ninety ships of war—just twenty-one of them steam powered! Dozens of ships needed fixing. So naturally, we set lickety-split to patching up hundreds of old ships and building new ones.

"But hold on!" exclaimed O'Keefe. "Our biggest

navy yard was Gosport. Here. On the Elizabeth River in Norfolk. Ah, lad, we lost it. And Virginia grabbed it. What do you think they got with that grab? Why, the biggest steam propeller ship in our navy, the *Merrimac*. But what do you think the Rebs are doing with her? Turning her into an ironclad!"

"Like ours?" I gasped.

"Tom," he whispered, "word is she's huge. Bigger than ours. A gigantic floating porcupine of bristling cannon, they say. And if she steams out and breaks the blockade, we're sunk."

He looked toward Ericsson's battery. "So what

The *Merrimac* when she was first built for the U.S. Navy.
At the time she had sails *and* a steam-driven screw propeller.

we're building here will have to stop that beast afore she comes out. Can you see now why what we're doing is so important? And why we're working so fast? Our iron-clad is being built to fight one ship: that *Merrimac*."

I glanced over to the flat, iron *thing* we were building. Seemed a tall order for such a . . . raft. "But . . . what's she going to fight *with*?" I ask.

"A turret."

"Mr. O'Keefe," I said, "what's . . . what's a turret?"

He leaned toward me and whispered into my ear, "Don't really know. See, the whole thing is supposed to be secret."

"Why?"

"Well, you wouldn't want them Rebs to know what we're doing, would you? Just hope the copperheads don't find out too much about her."

That made me jump. "What do you mean?"

"Just saying I suppose they'd give a bushel of gold to know what we're building."

I stared at him, wondering if he knew.

CHAPTER EIGHT

I Meet Mr. Ogden Quinn

I WAS WALKING HOME, not thinking about much of anything. Maybe dinner, because my stomach was growling. Hadn't eaten since coffee and bread that morning.

"Hey, Tom!" I heard.

Thinking it was some friend, I stopped and looked around. Right off I recognized that Rebel spy. He was standing in front of a café.

This time he had his hat in hand, so I could see his face. Narrow, with high cheeks. Long graying hair. Beneath his smallish nose, a droopy mustache. His smile was easy, but his eyes, even from 'cross the way, were fierce.

"How about something to eat?" he called.

I stood there, not sure what to do. My head filled with all kinds of thoughts: Just run away. We sure could use the money. The man's a traitor. But I also thought, I'm hungry. My father died for the Union—what did that get us? For sure, not much food.

I crossed the street.

"Glad to see you," said the man, holding his hand out for me to shake like I was a gent. "I was just sitting here eating when I saw you walk by."

I didn't believe that. I was sure he had been waiting for me.

"Come on in," he coaxed. "How about a steak?"

My mouth watering, I followed him into the café, a place crowded with workmen as well as gentlemen. Sawdust on the floor. Oil lamps on the wall. Waiters, napkins 'round their waists, scurried about with heavy trays. The smell of food was something fine.

"Take yourself a seat," said the man. It was a small corner table. He said he'd been eating, but no food was there.

I just sat there, barely looking at him and not talking.

"Bet you're hungry," he said. "Boys are always hungry. Work hard today?"

"Maybe . . ."

He grinned. "My name is Quinn. Ogden Quinn. And your name is . . . Tom. Right?"

I nodded.

"Tom what?"

"Tom."

An old waiter came up to us. "Evening, Mr. Parker," he said to the man who had just called himself Quinn. "What'll it be?"

"This boy needs a steak. A big, juicy one. Throw in a potato. That okay?" he asked me.

"Fine."

"Will do," said the waiter, and withdrew.

Mr. Quinn said, "He must have taken me for another fella." He laughed, but it sounded false.

I just looked at him, trying to get at what he wanted.

He sat back in his chair, returning my look with those sharp eyes of his. "Not much of a talker, are you?" he said.

"When I want."

Then, "How's that floating battery coming along?"

"Pretty well."

"You just see it?"

"Working on it."

His smile turned hungry. "Lucky you," he said. "Now, that steak will be here in minutes. Why don't you tell me about it?"

"The steak?"

"The battery."

I said, "How come you're talking to me?"

"You're smart-looking. See it in your face."

I just sat there, barely looking at him and not talking.

"But I'm just a boy."

"Pshaw, grown-ups can be stubborn. Boys are all go-ahead. They know a good thing. Your father employed at the Works?"

"He got killed."

"In the war?"

I nodded.

He pulled on a sad face. "Awful sorry to hear that. Terrible war. Terrible. You on your own?"

"With my mother."

He seemed disappointed.

Just then the waiter came back and put the sizzling steak and tater in front of me. They did look grand. "Anything for you, sir?" he asked Ogden.

"Not now." He waved the waiter away.

Instead of talking, I bolted food. Have to admit, couldn't remember when I'd eaten so good.

"Can I ask you some questions?" pressed Mr. Quinn, or Parker—whatever his name was.

"About what?" I said.

"That ironclad."

"I was told not to talk about it."

"By who?"

"Captain Ericsson."

He sat straight up. "You working for him?"

"Sure."

His eyes narrowed. "Calling her *Ericsson's Folly*, aren't they? I'd love to know more."

"I guess you would," I said, eating as fast as I could, avoiding his eyes.

"Just wondering how big her crew is. And her guns. How many? What kind? How fast can she shoot? That kind of thing." He reached into his vest pocket and brought up another gold piece. Laid it on the table. "I told you I had more of these, didn't I?" he said. "But look here, Tom." He pulled back his vest so no one in that café but me could see a holster strapped to his chest. In the holster, a pistol. On the holster he had affixed a copper penny, the one with "Lady Liberty" stamped on it: the symbol of the copperheads.

That killed my appetite. I said, "I don't know anything about those things."

"But you will, won't you?" He grinned, closed his vest, and nodded toward the coin on the table. "Go on. That's yours."

I looked down.

"But that other thing might be for you, too. And it wouldn't be so much fun, would it?"

I tried to swallow my meat.

"Well," he said, "how about it? Just tell me how many guns are on her."

"None," I muttered, grabbed the coin, and bolted out of the café. I could hear him laughing.

Before I got home, I decided I couldn't tell Dora I found another coin. She wouldn't believe it. Instead, I hid the coin out in the backyard under a stone.

As I walked up our steps, I found myself thinking of what my father might have said if he knew I'd taken money from a copperhead. None of it would have been pretty.

Not that I had told Quinn anything. In fact I told myself I had tricked him out of that money. Then why did having the coins make me feel so bad?

CHAPTER NINE

I Learn the Ship's Name

MOST TIMES SHIPS were given names of places, like the *Minnesota,* or something important, like the *Congress.* They named our ship the *Monitor.* Not that I knew what that meant.

Since Mr. O'Keefe seemed to know such things, I asked him.

"Captain Ericsson picked it," he said. "He wants to teach them Rebs a lesson!"

I thought for a moment. "I get it. A monitor—like a teacher."

O'Keefe grinned. "That's right. But here's the really important news going around. Remember that *Merrimac* I told you about?"

"The Confederate ironclad?"

O'Keefe leaned over and whispered, "Word

has it she'll be ready to sail by first of February."

"Will we?"

"Look for yourself."

I glanced toward the *Monitor*. She was sitting as still and flat as an iron bed—on land, too. No guns. No turret. Just men—almost two hundred—working like ants on a kicked-over anthill.

"Of course," said O'Keefe, "it's fine and dandy to name her the *Monitor*. But guess what the papers are calling her now?"

"*Ericsson's Folly.*"

"Where'd you hear that?"

I shrugged. "Just did."

"God willing, the *Monitor* won't be so full of folly as all that. Mind, we've got three things to do. First, we got to build her. Second, make sure she floats."

"What's the third?"

"See if she can fight."

"What's she going to fight with?"

"Guns."

"What if she can't?"

O'Keefe grimaced. "They say we'll lose the war."

He reached into his pocket and pulled out a folded sheet of newspaper. "Look here," he said.

The *Merrimac*

News from Fortress Monroe

A mechanic who came over under a flag of truce last evening furnishes us with some very valuable information in relation to the steam frigate *Merrimac*. He said her hull has been cut down to within three feet of her light-water mark, and a bomb-proof house built on her gun deck, and that she is not iron-plated yet. Her bow and stern have been steel clad with a projecting angle for the purpose of piercing a vessel. Her armament consists of four eleven-inch navy guns on each side, with a one hundred-pounder Armstrong at the bow and stern. She has no masts, and only a pilothouse and smokestack are to be seen above the bomb-proof deck. Her bomb-proofing is three inches thick and made of wrought iron. He states that she will not be ready for at least two weeks.

The *Merrimac* under construction as an ironclad.
The Rebs had a lot of trouble getting iron for her plating.

Later that day, I delivered a message from the Albany
Iron Works to Captain Ericsson. He was working on his
designs for the officers' cabins. The message was something about a change in the iron plate.

"Captain Ericsson, sir?" I said, after I gave him the
message.

"Yes, Tom," he said, without looking around.

"Something's been bothering me. It's . . . how can
iron float?"

The captain turned around and gazed at me. "Fair
question," he said. "When you put a ship in water it

pushes aside—we engineers say *displaces*—water. Pushing aside that water makes the water push *up* with its own force. If the force of the object pressing *down* is greater than the force of the water pushing *up*, the ship will sink. If the water's force is greater, the ship will float. Understand?"

"Sort of."

The captain continued, "A solid block of iron won't float. But a ship made of iron can float because it is hollow, filled with air. And air is less dense than water."

I thought hard. "So the ship just has to weigh less than the water it is pushing aside—I mean, displacing?"

"That's it."

I had to see it. So later, I found a tin can and took it down to the river. Laid it on the water. It floated. Then I took that same can and crushed it flat. When I put it in the water, it sank.

I felt smart. And knowing that the *Monitor* wasn't some crazy idea made me feel good about her, and even proud that I was working on such a modern ship.

CHAPTER TEN

I Battle for the *Monitor*

SATURDAY, my family went to our neighborhood church for a funeral. It was for Willie Hicks, a boy from our street. He had been in the same regiment Pa fought with, the Brooklyn Fourteenth. I don't think he was more than seventeen, but he was killed in some skirmish. He was cut up so bad they wouldn't open the coffin. I didn't want to go, but Ma said I had to. Made me upset to be there. Aside from Willie's death, it reminded me of Pa's.

After Mass, a few of my friends gathered on the sidewalk in front of the church. Sean Roberts was telling stories about Willie, how, on a dare, he once swam across the East River to Manhattan. It was sad talk, but then, like so often those days, the talk turned to the war.

"Can't wait 'til I join up," said Garrett Falloy, who was the biggest of us boys. "I'll teach them Rebs."

"I'm going to be a sharpshooter," said Sean.

"You hear about them balloon spotters?" said Luke Pator. "That's for me."

I got to saying what Captain Ericsson told me, that his floating battery—which I was working on—would win the war for sure.

"What's a floating battery?" Garrett demanded.

"Any fool knows a battery is a bunch of cannons," I said.

Garrett's father was a corporal in the army. And one of his uncles was a Brooklyn policeman. That and his size made Garrett sort of our street boss. He and I got on pretty well, but sometimes he used his bigness as an argument. So when I said "any fool," he snatched off his cap, flung it to the ground, and took a step toward me. "You telling me cannons can float?"

"If they're sitting on a ship, they will."

"On *Ericsson's Folly*?"

"She's called the *Monitor*."

"Made of iron, ain't she?" said Sean.

"Pretty much," I said.

"Iron can't float," said Garrett, giving me a shove. "Not nowhere."

"If the ship weighs less than the water it's displacing, it'll float."

"What's that supposed to mean?" said Luke.

Before I could answer, Garrett asked, "You sailing on her?"

"She don't sail. She's steam-driven. With a screw propeller."

"And you're screwy enough to go on her."

"I might," I returned, which was a *might* I hadn't thought of 'til then.

"You do," Garrett said, "and you'll be laid out like cold mackerel on Malachi's fish wagon."

"Right," hooted Luke. "We better start saving pennies for having Father O'Rourke say the drowned sailors' mass for you. Then we'll call your iron boat *Carroll's Folly!*"

The argument grew warmer, with me feeling bound to defend the ship as best as I could. Pretty soon all three of them were pushing me around. I began to hit back, not that I was a match for them.

Good thing Father O'Rourke stepped in. An old, white-haired man, he might not have been very big, but he had a strong grip and a stronger eye. "For shame! Your friend barely put to rest. Be off with you! Or you'll answer for it, first to me and then to God!"

I mean no disrespect when I say what sent them scurrying was mostly fear of Father O'Rourke.

"Let's go, Tom," he said, and with an arm around my shoulder, he led me away.

Pretty soon all three of them were pushing me around.

"Now, what's the trouble?" he asked when he got me alone.

"They were making fun of Captain Ericsson's ship, saying it won't float."

"That the iron boat they're building over at the ironworks at Greenpoint?"

"Yes, Father."

"What's that to do with you?"

"I'm working on her."

"Are you, now? Now tell me, Tom—man-to-man—do you think she'll really float?"

I sighed. "I'm sure she will, Father."

"We live in amazing times, we do," he said. "But even so, I'll offer up my prayers for added ballast. Now be off with you, and show some respect!"

Days were chilly, but we kept working on the *Monitor*. As soon as her decks were covered with iron, they painted her with white zinc paint, then black for color. Mostly they were working inside her now, not that it was any warmer below deck. Iron plating was cold!

I was doing what I always did: carrying orders, lugging pails, fetching tools, sometimes just holding things. And when I received my seventy-five cents each week, I gave it to Ma. It wasn't much, but she was grateful all the same, and took pains to praise me. I felt good about it, but wished I could make more. Still, I just couldn't touch those gold coins. It felt wrong.

Then Captain Ericsson made an announcement. Though the *Monitor* still didn't have her turret, he was going to send her down the ways and into the river. January the thirtieth.

That was in a few days.

CHAPTER ELEVEN

I Have a Meeting

WHEN WORD GOT OUT about the launch, there was nothing but talk about what might happen. Then Captain Ericsson—he being so sure of himself—announced that during the launching he'd be standing on the *Monitor*'s deck. I suppose in my head I did believe she would float, but I have to admit all that teasing left me uneasy. So I was glad I didn't have to be there.

But the day before the launch—it was almost quitting time—Captain Ericsson and I were alone in his drafting shed. He was working on his plans, making changes as always.

"Now, Tom," he said, as if he were going to ask me to fetch a telegram, "when the ship is launched tomorrow, I expect you to be by my side." He said it without so much as turning around to look at me. Or asking me what *I* wanted.

My stomach sank—not, I hoped, like the ship would. I felt some pride that he wanted me there. But for all my talk about how I was sure the *Monitor* would float, the idea of setting off on her made me jittery.

"Well?" he said.

"Yes, sir," I said, not knowing what else to say.

As if I didn't have enough to worry about, when I was heading out from work, I saw Mr. Quinn across the street. I knew he was waiting for me.

I hesitated, thinking I should head back into the Works. But the crowd of workers pressing out of the gates forced me on. Then I thought of stalling by talking to Luke, who was selling papers nearby. But he was real busy. Anyway, what could I say? The regular policeman was also there, but I was too scared to tell him what was happening. What if he thought I was a spy?

So, acting as if I hadn't seen Quinn, I started walking fast for home. Still, I knew he was behind me. After I'd gone a few blocks, I looked back. Quinn was nowhere in sight.

Feeling better, I slacked my pace but kept going, head down. I never wanted to see him again and was annoyed at myself for having taken his coins. And food. I knew why I did: we needed money. Even so, I wasn't going to have anything to do with copperheads. It was wrong. I'd rather be with Captain Ericsson. He wanted me by his side, and he didn't flash a pistol at me.

Just as I was feeling easy, I looked up. My heart lurched. Blocking my way was a grinning Mr. Quinn. How he managed to get there I never knew.

"You missed me," he said.

I took a quick look over my shoulder and saw another man—big and burly—come up behind me. I didn't even have to ask him what he was doing. I knew.

I took a quick look over my shoulder and saw another man—
big and burly—come up behind me.

I looked back to Mr. Quinn. He'd stopped smiling.

"Come on, Tom," he said. "We need to talk."

"Don't want to," I mumbled, trying to keep the shakes out of my voice.

"Now, see here, Tom. I guess you took my money, didn't you? You ate my food."

"I didn't make any deal."

"Hey, Tom, you're smart. I guess you know what I am. Suppose I got word to Captain Ericsson about us talking? What do you think he might do?"

"Don't know," I said, but I could guess.

"He'd hang you," he said. "You know that, don't you? Wouldn't matter that you were a boy."

I felt sick.

He said, "So why don't we just go off somewhere? I'll get you another nice steak. All you have to do is tell me what you've been seeing. Nothing but eat and talk. That's not going to hurt anyone, is it? I know about the launch tomorrow. It's what's inside her I'd like to know."

By this time, his friend had come up right behind me. I could feel him. Though breathing hard, I managed to say, "Can't stop now."

"Why not?"

"My . . . ma's expecting me. My sister's sick."

His eyes narrowed. "With what?"

"Coughing. Weakness. I'll talk to you tomorrow. After the launch."

His glared at me. "You sure?"

"Cross my heart and hope to die."

"You might," he allowed.

That made me sicker.

"And you promise to talk to me tomorrow when you come out of the Works?"

"Yes, sir," I said, unable to look at him.

He reached out and jerked my chin up so I had to look into his fierce eyes. "Tom," he said, "if you skip out, I'll find you. You know that, don't you?"

"Yes, sir."

"Just be there tomorrow," he said, and stepped aside.

Uncertain, I stood a moment, and then went forward. As I went by, he rapped me on the head, hard. It stung plenty and made me stumble, but I wasn't going to stop. Nope, I lit out and ran all the way home.

When I got there, I didn't go inside. I sat on the steps, smeared away my tears, and tried to think what to do. I felt cold inside. I couldn't believe I'd done anything so stupid as to listen to that copperhead.

I thought of running away. Anywhere. But I didn't want to leave home. Still, I knew I had to get some help. But not from my ma. Or Dora. Couldn't tell Captain

Ericsson, either. I sure wished my pa was there!

That made me remember: whenever I did something stupid, like not doing my paper route right, or sassing my sister, he'd say, "Hey, Tom, only way people are going to know you're smart is if you act smart."

That's when I thought of Garrett Falloy. Sure, sometimes he could be the bully. But other times he was a peacemaker. Not knowing anyone else I could go to, I decided I'd take the chance and talk to him.

CHAPTER TWELVE

I Go to Garrett Falloy

GARRETT LIVED IN ROOMS like ours, only four rooms instead of two. But he had a bigger family: he lived there with his ma, four sisters, and a two-year-old brother. Garrett was the oldest kid. And of course there was his pa, but he was away in the army.

As always, their door was open, so I walked into a small hallway. There were lots of voices coming from farther in. Garrett's youngest sister, Veronica, came running. She saw me, stopped, but didn't say anything. Just stared at me.

I said, "Got to speak to Garrett."

She wiped her nose with her fingers then bolted away.

"Garrett!" someone cried.

A few moments later Garrett came ambling out. He

had curly hair—all the Falloys had curly hair—and a red face with fat cheeks. When he looked me up and down, there was something of a smirk on his face. "What you want?" he said, so I suppose he was remembering that the last time we were together we had a bit of a scuffle.

I said, "Need to talk to you."

"About what?"

"I got some . . . trouble."

He grinned. "That floating battery sink?"

"It's going in the water tomorrow."

"You with her?"

"Not that kind of trouble," I said. "Copperhead."

He dropped his teasing look and peeked back down the hallway, as if making sure no one was there. Then he said, "Come on."

He led me around the corner to an old carriage house. The boys on the street often went there. It was like our headquarters. Only two of its brick walls were standing. The other walls were slanted boards.

We went to the back, where an unhinged door leaned against one wall. Garrett eased it open and went forward. I followed. He set the door back, leaving us in the dark and damp. Then he lit a safety match and set a candle burning.

The space was no more than ten feet square, but us

kids fixed it up like a small room. Even had a broken sofa, a three-legged table, and a chair.

Garrett threw himself down on the sofa while I stood before him. Then, "Go on, tell me."

I stood there—almost as if I was reciting in

The space was no more than ten feet square,
but us kids fixed it up like a small room.

school—and told Garrett what had happened. He listened through it all.

When I'd finished, he didn't say anything. Just pulled off his cap, rolled it up, and slapped one hand with it a few times. Then he said, "Why'd you even talk to that copperhead?"

"It was after my first day at the Works. He threw his money at me. With my pa gone, we don't have much. My ma does washing. So does my sister. But she's sick a lot." I shrugged. "So I just picked it up."

"Don't they pay you at the ironworks?"

"Seventy-five cents a week."

"Not much," he said, without smirking or anything. "What did the copperhead want from you?"

"Things about the *Monitor*'s guns. Crew. That sort of stuff."

"Did you tell him?"

I shook my head but recalled what Quinn had told me, that I could hang just for talking to him. Feeling tears well up, I said, "I thought I could just take his money. What am I going to do?"

"Just tell him . . . that the ship won't do cheese."

"Garrett, he showed me his pistol. Threatened me."

"That boat really important?"

"Going to win the war."

"Says who?"

"Captain Ericsson."

"The one who's building it?"

"Yeah."

"I could get my uncle, the cop. He lives close."

I shook my head. "I just want to keep Quinn away from me."

Garrett didn't speak for a bit. "What time you get off from work?" he asked.

"Seven."

"And you said you'd meet him tomorrow? At the gates of the Works?"

"Didn't know what else to say."

He thought for a moment. "There's two of them, right?"

I nodded.

"Okay. Go to work regular. And don't worry. By the time you come out—if you haven't drowned on that thing—I'll think of something."

"Thanks," I mumbled, and left. Right then, the only thing I wanted was for tomorrow to be yesterday.

CHAPTER THIRTEEN

I Ride the *Monitor* Into the East River

NEXT DAY — January thirtieth — launching day, came in cold but bright. I was pretty quiet over my coffee, bread, and molasses, thinking about all that was going to happen: the launching and Mr. Quinn. The way I was feeling, either way I would be sunk. In fact, I almost wished the *Monitor* would sink. That way I wouldn't have to meet Quinn.

When I couldn't put my going off longer, I hugged my ma good-bye. She was surprised, because I didn't offer too many hugs. But other than hug me back, she said nothing.

Just before I left, I got the gold dollar back from Dora, telling her I found out who had lost it. Then I fetched the one I'd hid in the backyard. If I met Quinn, I was going to make him take his money back.

Maybe Ma didn't know about the launch, but it was hardly a secret. Crowds of spectators had gathered at the ironworks to see what would happen. There were crowds across the river, too. Swarms of yard mechanics standing by to watch, cheer, or jeer, setting bets as to whether the *Monitor* would sink or not. Newspapermen were there. Artists were sketching the event for papers. There were even small boats close by on the river, ready to pluck off survivors if there came the sinking need.

I kept looking for Mr. Quinn, but I didn't see him.

Then it came: eleven o' clock in the morning. Launch time.

The *Monitor* was perched on smooth wooden skids, on an incline, held back by massive wooden blocks. Attached to our stern and then to the land was a heavy line. I supposed it was there to haul the *Monitor* back to shore if she sank. It made me feel better—and worse.

Some of the mechanics—my friend O'Keefe was one—stood by with huge hammers in hand, ready to knock the blocks away. The ship's weight was supposed to do the rest.

Captain Ericsson, wearing his top hat, stood midship near the place where the turret would be set. A few of his business partners were there, along with someone from the navy. I was, too, and not happy, my head full of thoughts about what I should do if the ship started to sink.

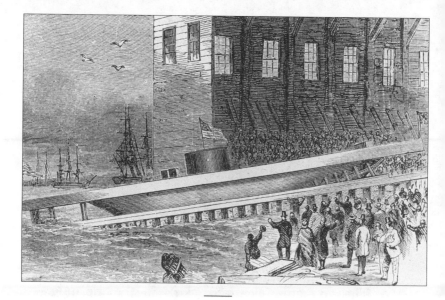

This picture had to have been made after the *Monitor* became famous, because at this time there was no turret on her.

I kept reminding myself I could swim, and that the water would be cold so I shouldn't be shocked. I told myself that the river was calm, with far less ice than before. At least I wasn't thinking about Mr. Quinn for the moment.

The only one not looking nervous was Ericsson. After a bit he cried, "Is all ready?"

"Ready, sir!" came the answer from the hammer holders.

"Hammers up!" I heard Mr. O'Keefe call.

Heart pounding, I forced myself to keep my eyes open.

Captain Ericsson lifted an arm and shouted, "Strike the blocks!"

There was a *crick-crack!* of hammer blows to the blocks. Next moment, the *Monitor* slipped down the ways, slow at first but picking up speed.

I was afraid to breathe.

Quick as winks, the *Monitor* slid into the cold river, spraying a fountain of foam, only to settle on the waters, wallowing like a fat duck. Then she—*floated!*—her deck only eighteen inches above the water! After 105 days of building—just a little behind schedule.

The crowd shouted, "Hurrah! Hurrah!"

I caught myself doing the same.

Captain Ericsson turned to me as if asking me a question.

"Displacement," I whispered.

For once he gave a real smile—which made me feel fine—nodded, and said, "All right then, Tom, there's work to do."

But as I followed him, I suddenly remembered: now I'd have to deal with Mr. Quinn. In fact, later that day, Mr. O'Keefe sidled up to me and whispered, "Hey, Tom, people are saying there were two Confederate spies watching the launch!"

That gave me a jolt. "They still here?"

"Didn't see them. If I did, I'd have wrung their necks."

As the day wore on I got more and more nervous.

How would I avoid Quinn? Would Garrett really help? Maybe I should go to his uncle, the policeman. But I was too scared to tell him what I'd done.

I considered confessing to Captain Ericsson. But by the time I got up my courage, he'd gone off to meet the newly appointed captain for the ship, John Worden. Then I thought of talking to O'Keefe, only to back off. I didn't want him thinking poorly of me.

Seven o'clock came too soon. The mechanics and laborers began streaming toward the gates. I started forward, stopped, and then went on. My hands were deep in my pockets, gripping those slippery gold dollars. My head was bowed—as if Quinn wouldn't see me if I didn't see him.

I went through the gates. I did see Luke, but no Garrett. No policemen either. Though my stomach was tight, I didn't dare stop. So I turned toward home.

And bumped right into Mr. Quinn. Bumped so hard I sort of bounced back. I jerked my head up, and there he was, smiling, but it wasn't any kind of smile you'd enjoy.

"Been waiting for you," he said.

I just stared at him.

"Saw you on that ship as she went into the water," he said, proving that it had been him at the launch. "We need to talk."

I pulled my trembling hands out of my pockets and

held out the dollars. "Don't . . . don't want these," I said. "And . . . I don't . . . don't want to talk to you."

"Now, Tom," he said, all easy, "that's not fair. You gave your word."

"Didn't," I muttered, and glanced over my shoulder. Mr. Quinn's friend was there. Awful close.

Mr. Quinn put a hand on my shoulder. Gripped it hard. "Tom," he said, "you promised."

I don't know where he came from, but suddenly Garrett Falloy came running.

Head down, he butted Quinn right in his guts. Did it so fast, so hard, the man reeled back as much from surprise as hurt. Same time, Luke came up and knocked into Quinn, too. That sent him down to the ground.

Before I realized what was happening, three other boys from my street—Jacob, Sean, and Connor—did pretty much the same to Mr. Quinn's friend—laid him flat on the street.

Once they were down, Garrett turned and grabbed my arm. "Come on, run!"

I took one step with him, then stopped and flung the dollars at Mr. Quinn.

Garrett halted. "You crazy?" He darted back, scooped up the coins, and then all of us—like a troop of cavalry—galloped off.

February 8, 1862

THE NEW YORK HERALD

SURRENDER
of Fort Henry
to Union Gunboats

DETERMINED RESISTANCE
OF THE REBELS

The Memphis and Ohio
Railroad Bridge
TAKEN

Official Report of
Commodore A.H. Foote
To the Secretary of the Navy

CHAPTER FOURTEEN

I Escape

THE FIVE OF US DASHED through the streets, a-whooping and a-hollering as if we'd won a great victory over the Rebs. Hadn't felt so good in a long time.

Garrett led us to the carriage house. There we did some more yelling, collapsed onto the sofa, laughed, and even wrestled a bit. We kept telling what happened maybe twenty times.

"Luke was our lookout," said Garrett with a grin. "Soon as he saw you with Quinn, he whistled us up. We were waiting."

Then Garrett plucked out the two gold dollars so all could see them on the palm of his hand. In the candle-light they glistened fine.

"Guess I got my reward, too," he crowed.

"You really giving them to Garrett?" Sean asked me.

"Ain't mine," I said with relief. "He's welcome."

"And Reb gold is still gold." Garrett laughed.

Then it was as if our fizz went flat. No one said anything for a moment. We just sat there. One by one, the other boys said they had to get on home.

"Thanks a lot," I called to each. Pretty soon it was just me and Garrett. He was still enjoying his dollars, flipping them up with his thumbs, catching them.

"Don't know what I'll do with these," he said.

"Do what you want," I said. Meant it, too.

"What are you going to do?" he said.

"About what?"

"Hate to tell you," said Garrett, all serious, "we got you away from them tonight. What about tomorrow?"

"What do you mean?"

"Tom Carroll, I reckon for a small chap you're the biggest fool. Don't you know they'll keep coming 'til they get you?"

My good feelings melted. "Guess so," I admitted.

"You better stay out of their way."

"Got to go to work," I said. "Need the money."

"You launched that ship today, didn't you?"

"It floated."

"She going off to station?"

"You bet."

"When?"

"Soon."

"If I were you I'd go with her."

"I'm not crew." Discouraged, I said, "Guess I better go home."

"I'll walk with you. In case."

I didn't refuse.

CHAPTER FIFTEEN

I Find a Place of Safety

IN THE MORNING, I figured I'd better find another way of getting to the ironworks. I made a big circle and came around opposite the way I usually did. The last two blocks I ran, racing through the gates.

I was awful glad to see Captain Ericsson in his shack when I got there. Soon as he saw me he said, "The turret's going on. And Tom," he added with his usual pride, "there's nothing like it in the whole world."

"I'm sorry, sir, I don't really understand what a turret is," I said, relieved to be fixing on the *Monitor* again.

Ericsson was only too happy to give an explanation. "First off, *turret* means *little tower*, like on a fort, only this one is all iron.

"Second, it's round—twenty feet across inside. Third, and best thing of all, it *turns* around."

"How?" I asked.

"The whole turret sits on a ring of brass. Right underneath the turret I've attached a strong shaft. I've designed a hand screw that lifts the turret up half an inch off that brass ring. That allows the turret to turn on the shaft. But what turns the shaft—and the turret—is a pair of steam engines down below. Inside the turret, there are levers to control those engines. What's it all mean? The gun crew, inside the turret, can control the turning of the turret."

"How fast?" I asked.

"Two and a half turns each minute."

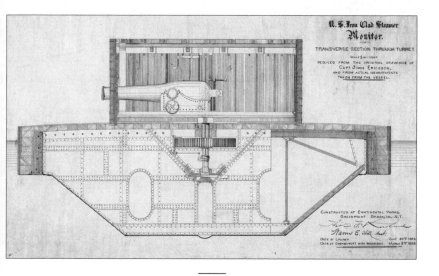

This is one of Ericsson's detailed plans for the turret.

Sure enough, that day they started putting the turret together. It was all iron plates, so they assembled it piece by piece, layering it like an onion. The plates were an inch thick, bolted together so each one could be removed easily if damaged. When they finished, the turret walls were eight inches thick!

Over the next several days, they put on the turret roof with its iron beams, reinforcing them with

This photograph of the turret was taken after the battle.
Look closely and you can see the dents made by enemy cannon fire.

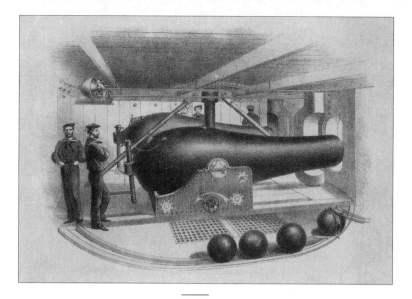

The turret looks pretty spacious here,
but during the battle there were nineteen men working in it!

diagonal braces. They covered the beams with *more* iron plate. Those plates had holes in them to let in light and air. Also, there were two escape hatches on top.

If I figured it right, from top to bottom that turret was nine feet tall, but because of how thick the iron was, only six or seven feet high inside.

In the turret, there was a wooden floor with four more hatches that could line up with other hatches in the deck below. That way, people could get in and out of the turret. You brought up cannon shot and powder bags the same way.

Was this whole thing heavy? One hundred and

twenty tons! And the guns weren't in her yet!

The turret had two gun holes. You rolled the cannons up to the holes with hand cranks and then fired.

Maybe the turret was like nothing else in the world, but even so, I was still thinking about *my* predicament. I just knew Mr. Quinn—a lot madder than before—would be waiting for me, with no Garrett to protect me. Truth is, I was getting panicky.

At quitting time, I started for the gates when Mr. O'Keefe came up alongside of me. "Hey, Tom," he hailed me. "How was your day?" he asked as we walked side by side.

"Okay," I managed.

"Remember my telling you about copperheads being at the launch?"

I stopped and looked up at him. "What about them?"

"Fellow over at smelting told me that they've been lurking around. Trying to find out about the *Monitor.*"

I didn't say anything, just kept walking. Then suddenly I stopped and blurted out, "One of them spoke to me."

Mr. O'Keefe stared down at me. "What did he say?"

I studied my feet. "He . . . wanted to know about the ship. Crew. Cannons."

"You tell him anything?"

I shook my head.

"He threaten you?"

That time I nodded.

Mr. O'Keefe was silent for a while, then he said, "I'll walk you to your home."

"Mr. O'Keefe, my ma doesn't know about this."

"Don't you think she needs to?"

I couldn't argue. In fact, I suppose I wanted her to know. "Neither does my sister."

"Sister now? You never said."

"She's older than me."

I took Mr. O'Keefe up the steps to our rooms. My mother, flustered with having a visitor, put aside the laundry she was working on. Dora was even more quiet than usual.

After I introduced them, I told my ma what I said to Mr. O'Keefe. I left out the money and the food. I was too ashamed. Even so, Ma became upset.

"Did you tell him anything?"

"Wouldn't."

"Do you think that man's going to come after you again?" asked Dora. The way she looked at me, I could tell she knew where that gold dollar had come from.

"Miss Carroll," said Mr. O'Keefe, "that's my worry. I was thinking Tom here might stay at the Works."

"Sleep there?" I cried.

"It won't be for long," said O'Keefe. "A month, maybe. Until the *Monitor* is gone."

"Would it be safe?" my ma asked.

"Men are there all hours, keeping the furnaces going," said O'Keefe. "Guards, too. No one could get at him."

Ma stared at her hands.

It was Dora who said, "Ma, I think Mr. O'Keefe's idea is right. Tom could sneak back from time to time."

"Won't need to sneak," said my friend, with a smile at Dora. "I'll bring him myself."

It was all agreed. But just before we left to go back to the Works, I sidled up to Dora and whispered, "I gave the money back."

She kissed my cheek.

Mr. O'Keefe walked me back to the Works. It was strange there. Not a lot of work was being done, though furnaces were glowing like hot, open mouths.

From somewhere, Mr. O'Keefe got me an old blanket.

"Where am I going to stay?" I asked as we moved toward the river side.

"The safest place there is."

"Where's that?"

"On the *Monitor*."

The pacing guard knew me, knew O'Keefe.

"Early for work, aren't you?" said the guard.

O'Keefe said, "Captain Ericsson wants him on board."

The guard waved us on.

We climbed into the turret. It was completely empty and smelled of cold iron. The floor was awful hard, and it wasn't exactly warm, either.

"Better sleep here," said O'Keefe. "Too much building clutter below deck."

Telling myself I wouldn't be staying there too long, I slept okay. Guess I was the first person to sleep on the ship.

But I suppose if I'd any idea what my staying there was going to bring, I might not have slept so well.

CHAPTER SIXTEEN

I Get a Surprise

NEXT MORNING I WOKE
early. It was strange being all
alone in the turret. Besides, I
was cold, stiff, and feeling
hungry. Still, I wasn't sure
whether to show myself or
not. When I heard someone
walking on the deck, I supposed it was Mr. O'Keefe. I
crawled out of the turret only
to come face-to-face with the
new captain of the *Monitor*, John
Worden. I'd seen him around,
but never met him.

He was a tall, thin man

Our captain, John Worden.
When he took command,
his beard reached his chest.

with a bushy beard. His skin wasn't nut-brown like most sailors, but pale as a high-class lady. That was because he had been the very first prisoner of war. Seems the Rebs grabbed him, said he was a spy, and kept him in jail—for *months*.

The Federals got him out, but when he came home to New York, he was sick. Even so, the navy offered him the job as the *Monitor*'s captain. (Those days the navy did not have a higher rank than lieutenant, but he was still captain of the *Monitor*, and we called him such.)

His family didn't want him to take it—not even when they learned that the pay was one hundred and fifty dollars a month! Despite bouts of fever, he took the position.

We looked at each other, both surprised.

"Who are you?" he asked.

"Tom Carroll, sir. Captain Ericsson's boy, sir."

"Ah, yes. I've seen you about. I'm Lieutenant Worden."

"Yes, sir. I know, sir."

"You're here early."

"Slept on board, sir."

"You must like her."

"Yes, sir, I do."

He eyed me as though trying to decide what to do with me. Guess he made up his mind, because he said, "Come with me."

I had to follow.

He marched down to the water's edge—me a step behind. It was blustery cold, the East River frothing with white-capped waves.

Waiting at the dock was a small boat with four sailors at oars. Worden got in. I stood by, watching. To my surprise, he told me to join him. I got in, too, and sat down, hardly knowing why he wanted me. He gave a command, and the boat set off downriver.

Feeling uneasy, I found my voice to ask, "Sir? Where we going?"

"We need a crew," he said.

"Yes, sir."

"Well, Tom—that is your name?"

"Yes, sir."

"There have been so many bad rumors about the *Monitor* that the navy is fearful about placing sailors on her. Afraid they will mutiny. I suggested I go to the *Sabine* and the *North Carolina*. They're full of sailors signed on for three years and waiting for assignments. I'm hoping they'll volunteer."

"But . . . why did you want me, sir?"

"You'll see."

Since he wasn't going to say any more, I just looked about.

New York City with all its docks had more ships

than I could count. Mostly sailing ships, though I saw some paddle steamers. I could see for myself how different the *Monitor* was. Made me kind of proud I was helping to build her.

Captain Worden, being expected on the *North Carolina*, was piped aboard. I scrambled up the rope ladder behind him. Not that anyone noticed me.

He was taken to the main deck, where the ship's commander welcomed him. Sailors were called up—maybe two hundred in all—out on the forecastle deck. A mixed lot, they were: all sizes, ages, colors. The one thing all those men had in common that I could see was their blue sailor's garb. Most were too young to have beards, but plenty of others did. Lots had tattoos.

They must have been told why we were there, because when Captain Worden climbed up on the capstan they listened to him with curiosity.

I was standing right below.

"Gentlemen," he began, "I am Lieutenant Worden, commander of the navy's ironclad, the *Monitor*. Newly made, she will shortly be off to her station in Hampton Roads, Virginia. There, one hundred miles from Richmond, the seat of the Rebel government, we'll defend our nation, secure the Union, and maintain our sacred liberties. I am here seeking a volunteer crew."

The sailors stirred, but just listened.

"I don't know what you've heard about the *Monitor*," Worden went on, "but I'm here to tell you that she's something entirely new to naval warfare—the likes of which has never sailed the seas before. Supported strongly by President Lincoln, she is the stuff of fame and glory. She's grand history yet unwritten. I promise you, she will do fierce battle. And I tell you just as honestly, the danger will be great. That said, I offer you a part to play and the inevitable thanks of a grateful nation."

Looking at him, I wondered if he meant what he said.

"Is she safe?" he continued. "That's the question all are asking. I would not command her if I thought otherwise. It was my choice. But of course we need a crew of brave character. So let me introduce you to the very first volunteer."

With that he reached down, and before I knew what was happening, he plucked me up from where I was. Made me stand before him.

"This is Tom Carroll. As you can see, he's only a boy. Yet he has volunteered to join me upon the *Monitor* as we go to sea and give battle to our enemy. He was so anxious to serve, he has already taken up quarters on her. Who among you will willingly join him?"

I didn't know if the captain truly thought I had

volunteered. All I know is after he spoke, there was a great cry of "Huzzah!" from the men. Nothing for me to do but just stand there and grin.

And *forty* men came forward to volunteer!

The captain gave the same speech on the *Sabine*.

By the end of the day, he had selected forty-eight men, mostly in their twenties. Depending on what they did on the boat, they'd earn between four to fifteen dollars a month.

When they signed on, many of them just wrote an X because they couldn't read or write. One man had the

"Who among you will willingly join him?"

same name as me. Two were freed-
men. Some were from faraway
places, like Ireland and England.
Even Sweden, where Captain
Ericsson came from.

Around the same time, the
navy named Mr. Dana Greene as
executive officer—second in command. Only eight years older than I
was! His deep black eyes and
hair made him look fierce.

Executive Officer Dana Greene.
There were those who
didn't like him, but
I found him a brave man.

Later, I found out the
names of some of the officers:
Isaac Newton (people told me he
was rich) was the chief engineer. He ran the main
engines, the ones that made us go.

Then there was Alban Stimers. Wasn't really part
of the crew. I think he was just watching over things for
his good friend Captain Ericsson. I liked his great mustache and big sideburns.

The paymaster was Mr. Keeler. He was from out
west somewhere and talked funny.

Dr. Logue was hired as our surgeon. When I saw
his bag of tools—saws, knives, and pincers—he scared
me plenty. Still, he was friendly enough and never
seemed to stop talking. Really annoyed Mr. Keeler.

And somehow a black-and-white cat got aboard and stayed. He was so long and lanky, someone named him Abe—after our president.

That was our crew. In all, thirteen officers and forty-five common sailors doing all kinds of duty: store men, firemen, clerks, cooks, coal heavers, stewards, and gunners. And that cat.

"Are you satisfied with your crew, sir?" I asked the captain the day after we had visited the *Sabine* and the *North Carolina.*

The *Monitor* officers. This photograph was taken soon after the battle, when Captain Worden was still in the hospital.

"I'm sure they'll be reliable," he said. "And remember, everyone has chosen to be there."

(Funny thing: though the sailors did volunteer, Paymaster Keeler told me later that some gave false names. That way they could jump ship if they didn't like it. No one would find them.)

Captain Worden cocked an eye at me and asked, "Will you be coming with us?"

"*Me*, sir?"

"Absolutely. You can go with the rank of first class boy."

"What's that mean?"

"You'll draw eight dollars in wages a month. Plus a uniform, two flannel shirts, socks, boots. Your own hammock and two blankets. All regular navy. You've already taken berth on the ship. You might as well stay. Just know, the *Monitor* will be heading south soon. What do you say?"

I hardly knew what to think. I had never been away from my family. If I joined the *Monitor*'s crew, I'd be the youngest. I'd be headed off to a real battle. Why, I might even get killed!

But then, I was already living on the *Monitor*, If I went out of the Iron Works onto the streets, I supposed Mr. Quinn would still be looking for me. Going on the *Monitor* meant I'd get away from Brooklyn and Mr.

Quinn. With all that iron plate on the *Monitor*, I might be safer on her.

And I'd helped build her. So I felt part of her. Since I was always there, always carrying messages, listening to Captain Ericsson, I knew all kinds of things about her. It even seemed Captain Worden *wanted* me to go. Eight dollars a month, too. My ma would like that part. Besides, the Navy would give me a uniform! And boots. A lot better than I was wearing. That was something, too.

In the evening, when Mr. O'Keefe came to make sure I was all right, he brought along a grand dinner: ham, biscuits, and red-eye gravy. I told him of Captain Worden's offer.

"Go," he said. "Be a fine chance for you. Might even be safer than staying."

That night as I lay in the turret wrapped in my blanket, I tried to make up my mind. There were lots of reasons to go, everything from the adventure of it to getting away from Brooklyn. As I thought it out, there was only one reason *not* to go: no one knew what would happen when the *Monitor* went off to battle.

When I realized the only way I'd really have the answer was by going, I decided to enlist. So there I was, Tom Carroll, first class boy. On the *Monitor*.

February 10, 1862

The New York Times

THE BURNSIDE EXPEDITION

The
ATTACK
upon Roanoke Island
Commenced

REPORTS RECEIVED FROM
THE REBELS

The National Forces Said
to Have Been Repulsed

CHAPTER SEVENTEEN

My Life Inside the *Monitor*

BEING CAPTAIN ERICSSON'S boy—and now part of the crew—no one thought it odd my living on the *Monitor*. Still, it was strange. After all, the iron deck sat just eighteen inches above the water like an iron tablecloth that draped over the ship's wooden hull. In other words, except for the deck and turret, the rest of the ship was *below* water. It was designed that way so there would not be much for the Rebs to shoot at.

Since the ship was mostly below water, the crew had to have air to breathe. Good air was pulled below deck by belted fans driven by steam engines. The same engines pumped out the bad air and smoke through deck funnels. In fact, there was an argument between

Captains Worden and Ericsson about those funnels. Worden said they weren't tall enough to keep off the high seas.

As always, Ericsson pulled up calculations to say otherwise. He wouldn't give way.

Worden, fed up, said, "Very well, sir: you build your vessel and I will sail her."

The navy wanted masts and sails on the *Monitor*. Captain Ericsson ignored that, too. We ran on steam, with a four-blade, nine-foot-diameter propeller. Ericsson had designed it. Pretty much the whole rear of the *Monitor* was for our engines, also designed by Ericsson. To run them we carried eighty tons of coal, enough for eight days. Engineer Newton told me our engines were like having four hundred horses working for us! But those engines were so loud, you heard *clank-clank* day and night. Like a heartbeat.

Another odd thing about the *Monitor* was her steering. There was a square pilothouse set near the bow. Boxlike, it stuck up from the deck just four feet. It was made of thick iron bars, bolted together and then covered with a two-inch iron plate kept in place by its own weight. Had these narrow slits—no more than half an inch wide—between bars. Those gaps were what allowed them to look out.

To get into this pilothouse you had to climb a ladder

from below deck. There was only room for the captain, who gave orders; a pilot, who would know local waters; and a helmsman, who steered with a six-spoke steering wheel connected to the stern rudder with ropes that ran through the ship.

In other words, on this whole, huge, iron ship, only the captain, the helmsman, and the pilot—squeezed tight—could see the outside world through a half-inch gap! That's why Ericsson had put in a speaking tube: so people in the pilothouse could talk to the turret crew.

The place where they made our food, the galley, forward of the engines, sat below the turret. It made me laugh to see the cooking stove. It was like what you might see in a home.

Inside the *Monitor* it was dim, even gloomy, with only a little light from hanging oil lamps. There were these tiny windows, small disks of heavy glass set into the deck. They helped, but only during the day.

All her thick metal made the ship hot during the day and cold at night. Let me tell you, we either sweated or near froze.

Of course, the whole crew would live *beneath* the deck, sharing space with powder and shot. The place where the crew would sleep, called the berth deck, was just seventeen feet below the top of the turret. There was a sixteen by twenty-one foot space, where forty-nine of

The berth deck felt much smaller and much more crowded
than what is shown here.

us would sleep in day/night batches. There were little
lockers for private things.

But it was hardly private. One of the crew showed
me spy holes in the wall between the crew and officer's
space. I guess the officers planned to keep watch on us.

Officers would eat in their own quarters on a fancy
table with fine white china. There even was a butter dish
with the ship's name on it. But each officer had to bring
his own forks and spoons.

The eight officers, with their servants, had their
own rooms. The rooms might have been small—six feet

by eight—but they had fancy beds, rugs, air registers, black walnut trimming, brass fixtures, storage closets, desks with drop-down lids, and washbasins.

Who designed it all? Captain Ericsson. He paid for it, too.

Captain Worden had *two* rooms. In one of them he kept some navy books: *Nautical Almanac, Bache's Tide Tables.* The one I liked was *Piddingham's Book on Storms.* Had good pictures.

There were toilets below—"heads," sailors called them. Being underwater, they were operated by pumps. *Another* Ericsson invention. To use these heads, you closed one valve, opened another, then worked a pump to get rid of waste.

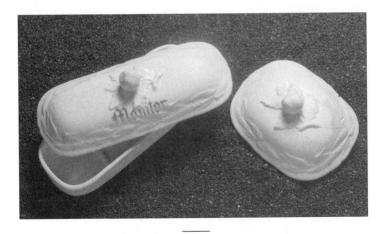

The officers' butter dish. The lettering was made with real gold!

Early on, one of the coal heavers didn't use the valves right, and he was blown off the seat! He complained to Captain Worden, but only got laughter for his trouble.

Walls between quarters were thin and didn't even reach the ceiling, so as to allow for airflow. Doors could be closed, but conversations weren't private. So as I walked about, I would often hear, "When will we be done? When will we get going? Ain't the *Merrimac* complete? Ain't that Reb boat ready to burst out?"

What we did know was that the *Merrimac* was ready, willing, and able to attack the Union blockade in Hampton Roads. We needed to get down there. Fast.

March 1, 1862

THE PHILADELPHIA INQUIRER

IMPORTANT
WAR NEWS

Evacuations of Columbus, Kentucky

Occupation of Nashville

Jeff Davis's Message
to the Rebel Congress

The War in Arkansas

LATEST FROM
FORTRESS MONROE

CHAPTER EIGHTEEN

We're Almost Ready

NOT A DAY PASSED without Captains Ericsson or Worden getting telegraph messages from the Department of the Navy. Constant reminders that the *Merrimac* was going to appear in the Hampton Roads, and was going to wreck the Feds' Blockade Squadron. "Work faster!" they urged. "We must have the *Monitor* on station!" A note came saying even Mr. Lincoln was worried.

One day, I carried Ericsson a slightly different message from the navy: "It's very important that you should say the *exact* day the *Monitor* can be at Hampton Roads."

Ericsson scribbled an answer: "Soon."

There wasn't exactly panic at the *Monitor*. But folks were sure worried that the *Merrimac* would be attacking before we could get down there. So work on the *Monitor* went all the time, day and night. I wasn't alone at night anymore. If anything, it was too noisy.

At last they put our guns in place. We got two eleven-inch smoothbore Dahlgren cannons, taken from the USS *Dacotah*. New, too, cast in 1859. They were thirteen feet long and weighed more than eight tons *each*! Our gunners called them "soda pop guns" because of their shape: big bulb at the back part—the breech. The two were placed side by side, set on rolling carriages with brakes to reduce recoil.

Ball shot was set up in gutters around the guns. Gunpowder was off to one side. More was stored under the turret. Powder and shot had to be passed up through floor hatches. Lifting the powder bags wasn't hard, but we had to use a metal grip attached to a pulley system to haul up the heavy cannon balls—one hundred and sixty-five pounds each!

It took almost eight minutes to load and shoot each cannon. After a shot went off, the cannons had to be sponged out with a soaking-wet mop. That cooled the iron. You couldn't place a new charge in the cannon if it wasn't cool and all sparks quenched. Otherwise, when you put in powder it might explode.

There even was this thing called a worm—a wire looking like a pig's tail that plucked out any bits of the old powder bag. Finally the cannon was stuffed and rammed with a new bag of powder, then loaded with the cannonball, the whole charge packed in tight as a fist. All this was done through the muzzle.

When ready to shoot, the cannons were run out one at a time through the two-gun ports, using hand cranks. When the firing lanyard was yanked, those guns could throw the shot ball more than a mile!

Then the guns had to be pulled back, swabbed cool, loaded, and charged with powder again. When that happened, the gun ports were closed with a crazy system of shutters so heavy it required lots of men to work them.

It took four days to get the guns properly lined up. Still, during the first practice firing—without shot—the guns fell off their carriages. God's blessing no one was killed.

Finally, our boilers were fired up. Engines clanking, we cast off. Guess what? The engines had been set for reverse. We slammed back into the dock!

Talk about panic. Not from Captain Ericsson, though. Said he'd make adjustments. In two days he did. Heck, far as I could see, Captain Ericsson could think us to the moon if he wanted to.

Things began happening even faster.

February thirteenth, news came that down in Virginia the *Merrimac* had been launched.

On the fifteenth, a telegram came for Captain

Worden. I ran it to him. He was in his rooms with Executive Officer Green.

"An urgent telegraph, sir." I gave it to him.

Mr. Green and I waited as the captain read the message. "From the Department of the Navy," he said. "It reads, 'The *Monitor* is wanted *now*!'"

Captain Worden sighed. We weren't going anywhere.

The nineteenth, in the afternoon, the *Monitor* was turned over to the United States Navy, and we got her official flags. That meant Ericsson was no longer in charge of her.

That same day, we went from Greenpoint to the Brooklyn Navy Yard, adding a trial run around New York Harbor. Just in case, a tug followed. Good thing, too, because our boilers didn't work well. The *Monitor* went too slow, only three and a half knots. At Governor's Island we came about and didn't get to the Navy Yard 'til early evening.

Not good.

Work continued, mostly on the ship's engines.

On February twentieth, the Secretary of the Navy sent Captain Worden another message:

Proceed with the USS Monitor, *under your command, to Hampton Roads, Virginia.*

We loaded eighty tons of anthracite coal along with all our ammunition. But we didn't go anywhere. We were still finishing or fixing things. Wasn't 'til the twenty-fifth that the navy officially took possession of the ship.

Two days later—it was snowing—a navy pilot came on. We nosed out into New York Harbor. The hatches were pulled down so we were all below deck. All around was hard, cold iron. There was a strong stink of iron and sweat. Murmuring voices. Gloomy light and a constant *clank-clank* of the main steam engines.

Moving down the calm East River, we hardly felt motion at all. Maybe a slight tipping and rocking back and forth. It all made me remember what that guard had called the ship: an iron coffin. But with the air blowers doing okay, we had no trouble breathing.

I had a thought: in the whole world there was no other ship like this *Monitor*! And me, Tom Carroll, the only boy in the whole world upon her! The idea popped up goose bumps on my arms.

Except, the steering wheel proved too small. The *Monitor* started bouncing around, from Manhattan to Brooklyn and back like a three-wheeled buggy. We even rammed a dock—a riverside gasworks near the Fulton Street Ferry. We were towed back by steamer tug.

Captain Ericsson had to fix us a bigger wheel.

So there we were in the East River, still going nowhere. The closest we got to excitement was sitting 'round while one of the crew read a book, something called *Waverly*. Too many words for me.

Then we got a telegram from Washington that said the *Merrimac* was about to attack.

And we were still in Brooklyn.

CHAPTER NINETEEN

We Make Our Final Preparations

WITH MECHANICS STILL WORKING on the ship, and the whole crew on board, quarters were very crowded. Bad weather kept us below deck, but people felt uncomfortable having no sky overhead. Not knowing each other, it took time for the sailors to get along, too. In other words, everyone was getting edgy.

March third, we did some test shooting with blanks. Trouble was we had to stop the final test run of the ship because it was raining too much. We learned then that the ship leaked. No one had dry feet on the *Monitor*.

Next day we made another run. I squeezed into the pilothouse, where the captain, the helmsman, and a harbor pilot were stationed. Standing on a small platform, Captain Worden pressed his face against the gaps between the iron bars to see where we were going. He kept shifting his position, looking first one way or another, trying to get his bearings.

Mr. Geddings, the harbor pilot, knew the New York harbor as well as any man. "This is the most curious view I've had from any ship I've sailed. You're awful low in the water," he said. "Think you can see enough?"

"It will do," the captain said.

"For a battle?" Mr. Geddings asked.

Captain Worden didn't answer.

"For a battle, sir?" Mr. Geddings asked again.

The helmsman waited for the answer. I waited, too.

After a moment, Captain Worden said, "It will suffice." Then he ordered, "Take her into the Lower Bay." He turned to me. "Tom, come with me."

We climbed down the ladder, worked our way back past the officers' quarters, into the storerooms beneath the guns. I looked up through the grating. I could see the feet of gun crew, the underside of the great cannons.

The passageway to the turret was open, so we went up the ladder. Inside the turret, the gun crew was still trying to find an easy way to shift the heavy shutters that covered the gun ports.

There was another ladder that led to the turret's roof. Captain Worden climbed out, then reached down to help me up. Standing on the turret top in the cold rain, I could see that we were out of the East River and

Inside the turret.
During the battle there were a lot of men stationed in her.

into New York Bay. We were going about seven knots in calm waters. Any number of ships were about. As we steamed along, lots of people watched us. We must have appeared something strange.

"Come along," the captain said. He climbed down the outside ladder to the black deck. My feet could feel the steady pulse of the engines. Now and again a small wave curled over, making the deck slippery. I thought,

This must be like riding the back of a whale.

I stayed by the turret, wet spray in my face as the captain went forward—skirting the pilot box—until he stood at the bow, one hand holding on to the fluttering navy-jack mast. He remained standing there, not moving. I had no idea what he was thinking. It looked like he wanted to be alone. But then he beckoned to me. Walking wide to keep my balance, I drew up. He put a hand on my shoulder, and we gazed over the bay.

"Tom," he said, "one of the things a captain faces is that he's not always free to speak his mind."

I stared out over the water.

"But sometimes it's easier to talk to the young."

"Thank you, sir."

"So you'll hear it from me now—and never again. Do not repeat what I am about to say. Tom, I've been in the navy since 1834—a midshipman at the age of sixteen—and have answered many a call on many a ship, but this is the strangest vessel I've ever sailed."

I looked up into his bearded face. He was somber. "Do you doubt her, sir?"

"Not the ship, Tom. Myself."

"How so, sir?"

"I'm forty-three years of age—and have been ill. I ask myself if I am ready for such newfangledness."

He put a hand on my shoulder, and we gazed over the bay.

"I think so, sir."

The captain smiled. "If youth says so," he said, "it must be!"

"Are we going south, then, sir?" I asked.

"We are. Very soon."

Suddenly we heard a rumbling. Turning, we saw the turret moving. Amazing to see it—so huge. Next moment, the gun ports opened and a cannon was run out—aiming right at us.

"Sir!" I cried.

"Don't worry," he said, laughing. "I'm sure they know we're here. But, Tom, I must tell them they mustn't shoot the guns over our bow."

"Why?"

"They will blow the pilot box—with me in it—to smithereens."

When we reached Sandy Hook, the guns were tested, firing blank charges. All went well.

That night, asleep on the *Monitor*, I dreamt of great dark whales, swimming deep. I was trying to ride one.

CHAPTER TWENTY

The Night Before Departure

MARCH FOURTH WE MADE our last trial run, including cannon firing. Things went well, except when we got back to the Yard, Paymaster Keeler discovered that two seamen had deserted. Took a dinghy, too—one of the ship's small rescue boats. They must have fled across the river to New York.

There was lots of talk in the sailors' quarters. People wondered if the two got scared, found better berths on other ships—or were spies. A coal heaver said, "Whatever they were, we're better off without."

I thought different. If they were spies, it might mean Mr. Quinn knew we were about to head south. If so, he'd really want to grab hold of me to hear what I knew, which was a lot. And the thing was, before we went, I had to get home to Ma and Dora. I just couldn't go without saying good-bye. I might never see them again. And with the weather clearing, everybody was hoping we would leave in the morning.

At quitting time I went out to the main Navy Yard gates. Garrett was there, selling papers. I ran up to him.

"They say we're leaving tomorrow. I'm not sure, but I have to get home. If Quinn's going to grab me, it'll be tonight."

"Don't worry," he said. "I'll fix things."

"How?"

"I'll do something," he said. "When you want to go?"

"In an hour."

Then I discovered that Captain Worden decided he would hold a farewell dinner on ship. That wouldn't ordinarily be a problem for me, but the cook got drunk, so Worden put him in the brig. That meant *I* had to do all the serving alone. Now I really wanted to get home, but I didn't know when I could.

All the officers were at the dinner. So was Captain Ericsson, though word was out that he wouldn't go. Seemed that when he first came to America he got seasick. Wasn't about to go to sea again! Made me laugh. And then during dinner, Captain Worden announced we were leaving in the morning—for certain.

"Is this a secret, sir?" asked Paymaster Keeler.

"Let's hope so."

Once dinner was over I rushed to clear everything away. Then I went to Captain Worden's quarters. When I got to the door I overheard Mr. Greene, the second in command, speaking.

"I tell you, Captain," Greene was saying, "there never was a vessel launched that needed more trials. No part of her is finished. Not even the gun ports have been rounded smooth."

Captain Worden said, "We'll have to take our chances, Mr. Greene. We can't wait anymore. We're needed."

A silence followed, so I knocked on the door. Got permission to enter.

"Yes, Tom?"

"Sir, request permission to go ashore to say good-bye to my ma and sister."

"Where are they?

"Not far from the Yard, sir."

The captain exchanged a look with his executive officer.

"Not planning to fly off, are you?" said Mr. Greene, looking at me with his fierce dark eyes. "Like those others?"

"No, sir, I wouldn't. On my honor, sir!"

Captain Worden pulled a brass pocket watch from his jacket and looked at it. "Tom, I'll give you two hours. Be back by midnight."

"Yes, sir. Thank you, sir."

I leaped off the *Monitor* to the wharf, tore through the Yard, out through the gates, and onto the Brooklyn streets. Once there, I stopped and looked around. Everything was deserted, dark, and cold, a stiff breeze coming off the East River. A few streetlamps were glowing and only a couple of lights in house windows. But no Garrett.

Telling myself I needed to go only a few blocks, I set out. I'd barely gone a block and a half when I heard something. A scraping sound and a low whistle. It came from behind me. Wasn't much, and I hardly thought it was worth any worry. Even so, I ran faster, keeping to the middle of the street.

Then I heard another whistle. From in front of me, this time.

I stopped and peered into the dark. Another whistle from behind made me look back. Then down the street, before me, a man appeared. I looked around. There were two men behind me. By the time I whipped 'round to look ahead again, there were another two men. One of them passed beneath the gas streetlamp: Mr. Quinn.

My stomach rolled.

"Tom?" he called. "That you? Fancy meeting you here."

I stood where I was, but the men kept coming toward me.

"Now, Tom," I heard Mr. Quinn say, "I've had enough of your putting me off."

The men behind me came up quickly. One of them grabbed me by the neck. Another took my arm.

Mr. Quinn stood before me. "All right, Tom," he said. "Now, just come along."

They started to march me away.

Suddenly, I heard "Charge 'em!" And from different places and directions maybe six policemen came rushing in, yelling, "Get them copperheads! Catch them Rebs!" Lights went on in windows along the street. That's when I saw that Garrett was there, too.

Quinn's men tried to escape, but the policemen quickly surrounded and collared them.

Garrett grabbed my arm and led me up to one of the policeman. "This is my uncle Mike," he said to me. He was a big man, and looked a lot like Garrett's father, curly-haired and red-faced.

"Uncle Mike, this is my friend I told you about," Garrett announced.

"Which one is the Reb who wanted you to spy?" the policeman asked me.

"That one," I said, pointing. "He calls himself Quinn, but he may be Parker, too."

"If you're going to take me," Quinn snarled, "you'd better take the boy, too. He works for me."

"Don't listen to him, Uncle Mike," cried Garrett. "I told you, Tom's the one who found him out."

"Right enough. But you'll need to make a statement

"He calls himself Quinn, but he may be Parker, too."

at headquarters," the policeman said to me.

"Please, sir," I said, "I'm sailing with the navy tomorrow morning. The *Monitor*."

"Are you, now?" the policeman said, looking me over with new interest. "Then we won't be able to hold them. But hopefully it'll give them a scare. And we can keep watching them. But if you're sailing in the morning you'd better skedaddle!"

With that, the policemen marched off with Mr. Quinn and his friends.

Garrett and I watched them go. Feeling enormously relieved, I turned to my friend. I said, "I thought he had me for certain."

"Then they wouldn't have been able to sail the *Monitor*, right?"

Not able to do much else but grin, I said, "We'd better get going."

We went toward my home. When we got to the door, Garrett said, "Are you going to visit?"

"Just a bit. Got to get back to the boat."

"I'll wait."

I tore up the steps and into our rooms. Ma was in the kitchen, working. Her irons were heating on the stove.

"Tom!" she cried, when I burst in.

Standing there, suddenly not knowing what to say, I managed, "I . . . I wanted to say good-bye."

She stared at me. "Are you really leaving?" There had been tears when I told her I was joining the crew. But when I explained my reasons, she thought it was the right thing to do. Now her eyes were full of sadness.

"In the morning," I said. "If the weather holds."

She continued to stare at me without saying anything. Then she went and fetched Dora from the other room. I think my sister had been sleeping.

"Going, Tom? Truly?" Dora said.

I nodded.

"To a battle?" Ma whispered.

Full of brag, I said, "Hope so."

They stood there gazing at me as if I were something strange. Maybe it was my uniform. It was too big for me, with baggy trousers and overlong arms—all turned up.

Then my ma gave me a hard hug and a kiss on my head. "God protect you and keep you safe," she said. Dora did as much.

"Don't worry," I said, "I'll come home."

I guess we were all thinking of Pa.

I didn't know what else to say, but had to work to keep my eyes free of tears. "I have to go back," I muttered, and turned away.

Ma called after me. "Tom. Honor to your father's name!"

I ran back and hugged her.

I ran back and hugged her. "Promise!" I said, and tore down the steps.

Garrett was waiting. The two of us ran back to the Yard. At the gates I stopped.

"Thanks" was as much as I could say.

Garrett punched my shoulder. "Hey! Make sure you win the war! For Brooklyn!"

I grinned and said, "I will!"

He headed off, and I went back to the *Monitor*.

As I got into my hammock on the crowded sailors' deck, I hardly knew what I felt. Excitement, pride, fear, and, though I hadn't gone yet, a lot of homesickness.

Lying there, I could hear mechanics still working on the ship. They would do so right up to the hour of our departure.

I remembered the captain's words: *No part of her is finished.* And I thought, Same could be said of me!

Yet we were both going—for sure.

March 5, 1862

The Tri-Weekly Telegraph

Important from Nashville!

The Federals Not Yet in

POSSESSION

Fayetteville DESTROYED

Confederates at

BOSTON MOUNTAIN

Battle Imminent

AT CUMBERLAND GAP

CHAPTER TWENTY-ONE

I Say Farewell to Brooklyn

MARCH SIXTH, FIVE A.M., the whistle sounded. Then the cry came: "All hands up hammocks!"

It was slow going at first. But excitement grew when, the weather checked and it being clear and bright, we knew we were really going to cast off and head south.

There was lots of uproar as everyone rushed through duties. I served officers their coffee and oatmeal. Everyone ate fast.

I helped put up our six-foot travel funnel atop the main engine stack and the four-foot funnel on the air blower stacks. As I helped remove the turret awning, the boilers down below were blooming with full heads of steam. The engines were clanking. Our thirty-four-star

This picture of the *Monitor* shows deflecting shields on the pilothouse.
They were added after the battle.

United States flag hung from the stern while the navy jack—just stars—was at our bow. The commission ensign was atop the turret.

By nine o'clock we all were at our stations.

We were ready.

Captain Ericsson came aboard and sat with Captain Worden in the captain's quarters. I had no idea what they said since I was helping to stow gunpowder sacks in the magazine. But as Captain Ericsson was leaving, he came through where I was, paused, and shook me by the hand.

"So you go at last, Tom," said he. "Godspeed."

"We'll lick them, sir," I said. "I know we will."

"Of course," he said. If any man had more confidence in the *Monitor* than Captain Ericsson, he wasn't of this world.

I went with him as he returned to the deck. As he stepped off, the navy pilot, a Mr. Miller, whose job it was to guide us through the narrows of New York Harbor, came on.

Miller joined Captain Worden in the pilot box, along with the helmsman. Orders were given to cast off.

Thing was, right up to then, men were still working on the ship. I saw one man stuffing oakum in the crack beneath the uplifted turret. Oh, if I'd only understood what that would mean!

About ten thirty in the morning we threw off our mooring ropes. Propeller churning, turret screwed down on its brass ring, we eased away from the Navy Yard docks and into the East River.

We were going at last! Maybe the crew was calm, but I'd never been more excited.

I guess everybody did know we were going, because when we pulled from the Yard, we saw crowds of people watching us from both banks of the river.

When the *Monitor* slid down into the water that first time, the crowds had been cheering and shouting. But there we were, finally sailing off to save the Union, and I didn't hear the smallest hoot of applause—just silence.

I guess they didn't think we could do much.

We moved out of the East River, passed the Battery, and cruised into Lower New York Harbor, then through the Narrows. Four ships joined us: two armed paddle steamers, the *Sachem* and the *Currituck*, to give protection as we headed south; a cutter to bring back the harbor pilot; and the steam tug, the *Seth Low*, keeping close in case we got into trouble.

When we got to Sandy Hook, off New Jersey, we paused. The cutter came, and the pilot took his leave.

Captain Worden thanked him with a handshake. "Mr. Miller," he said, "may I request that when you get back to the Yard in Brooklyn, you send a telegraph to the Department of the Navy. Tell them that we are well off and heading for Hampton Roads."

Mr. Miller said he would, and took his leave.

Then the captain had us signal the *Seth Low*. Because the *Monitor* was going so slow—only five and a half knots—he asked the tug to take us in tow so we could go faster. A four-hundred-foot rope was attached, and we moved better. Soon we were in the ocean. All sight of land was gone.

"Please, sir," I said to the captain, "can I go atop the turret? I've never seen the ocean."

The captain's eyes rested on me with interest. "I'll go with you," he said.

Soon as I climbed out and looked around, I was stunned: the sea was so huge it drew my breath away. In all directions the rolling iron-colored waves made me think of our ship being held in molten iron! The *Monitor* seemed so tiny.

Under tow, the *Monitor* moved steadily. The weather was clear, if cold; the sea easy. As I stood atop the turret, the sun went down, becoming huge before it vanished. A pale moon rose, shining light bright enough to see white sails of distant ships. Closer in were the green running lights of the *Sachem*, the *Currituck*, and the *Seth Low*. We weren't so alone after all.

The paddle-steamer tug, the *Seth Low*,
which towed us from New York down to Virginia

"Well, Tom," the captain said. "What do you think?"

"Sir, I'm feeling pretty small."

"Tom," he said, "on the sea, I assure you, everything is untried and unknown."

"Do you mean the *Monitor*, sir?" I asked.

"The ship and us," he said.

By way of celebration, a fine dinner was provided for the officers' mess. The cook stayed sober. Though Captain Worden was not feeling well—a touch of his prison fever—he was jolly, telling tales of his midshipman days.

At that moment I wanted nothing more than to spend my life at sea.

During dinner that first evening, Chief Engineer Newton proclaimed he'd never experienced a vessel easier on the sea. No one disagreed. It was true: the motion of the ship was such that nothing on the table so much as shifted a hair.

By eight thirty, the *Monitor* reached Barnegat Light. A little later, the first watch—including me—turned in. Within the crew's berth, it felt like twilight, the only light coming from dim, rocking lamps. Our lights went out at ten p.m. It was warm and close below. I could hear the constant splash of waves washing over our deck. The steady *clank-clank* of our engines lulled me. Abe, the cat, meowed once.

Captain Worden went atop the turret. The iron top being like a drum, I could hear him pacing restlessly above, his sound mixing with the ever-clanking engines. I felt as if I were in another world.

We had no communication with anyone on shore. That's why we did not know that two hours after we left Brooklyn, an urgent telegraph had come from Secretary Wells of the Department of the Navy.

We were *not*—he said—*not* to go to Hampton Roads and fight the *Merrimac*. We were to go to Washington instead.

The other thing we didn't know: it was learned that a Rebel spy in New York had sent word south that we were on our way.

For now, all we knew was that we were heading for Hampton Roads through the iron-gray Atlantic sea.

CHAPTER TWENTY-TWO

Disaster!

I SLEPT. BY THREE in the morning we'd passed by New Jersey's Atlantic City. Six in the morning—March seventh—when my watch was called, I lay in my hammock thinking, How easy this is! Then I got up, helped stow things, and went to get coffee for the officers.

But it wasn't long before a gale started blowing from the east. Didn't just blow, either. It roared. In ten minutes, that storm had turned things from calm to fury. Pounding rain. Howling wind. High seas. The *Monitor* began to tip violently. It was as if we'd been ambushed. There was nothing to do about it, either; just wait it out with an awful feeling of helplessness.

With the *Monitor* lurching, shaking, and trembling, lots of the crew got seasick. Even the captain, in his rooms, was ill. But the storm only got worse. Waves grew bigger, stronger. It was hard to walk. I couldn't think of anything but the next heave of the ship—and my guts.

It got so violent that water shot through the pilot-house viewing slots and knocked the helmsman over. I leaped to the wheel and tried to keep her steady. Couldn't, really. The soaked helmsman dragged himself up and took over again.

More and more water began to slosh underfoot. Shoes and boots got soaked. Looking up through the windows, all I could see was the green sea washing over the deck. I swear I saw a fish!

Everybody was miserable. The ship stank of sickness and nervous sweat. The one place that stayed warm and dry was the engine room, but it hardly had any space.

Our misery was nothing to what happened next. Remember how I'd seen a workman stuffing oakum into that half inch of space between the deck and turret just before we left?

This is the way it was explained to me later: oakum—strands of twisted hemp mixed with tar—is what sailors use to fill cracks in boats to prevent leaks. See a crack in a ship—stuff it with oakum. It's what sailors *always* do. They use it so much it stains their fingers black. That's one of the reasons sailors got to be called "tars."

Now, the way Ericsson designed his turret, there was no crack. It was so heavy it just squeezed down, watertight. But just before we left, it had been screwed up—for fresh air—making a half-inch gap. When that fellow saw the gap, he stuffed oakum in it. That kept the gap *open*. When the storm came, seawater began pouring into the *Monitor* like some Niagara Falls.

Yes, the *Monitor* had water pumps driven by our engines to deal with leaks. But there was so much water coming in, the pumps couldn't get it out fast enough.

Water in the ship started rising.

We brought out hand pumps. Not much use.

Water kept rising.

Mr. Greene organized a bucket brigade. There were too few pails. Besides, passing sloshing pails from the bottom of the boat, up the ladders, through the turret—seventeen feet—barely worked.

The water kept rising.

Even worse happened. Remember how I said there were air funnels for our engines? The ones that stood over the engine just in back of the turret? The main smokestack standing six feet tall? Air-system funnels four feet high? Since we were mostly submerged, we *had* to have fresh air coming in for the coal-fired engines to work and for us to breathe. Those engines pushed out *bad* air, too.

Water in the ship started rising.

But Captain Worden had been right. The funnels weren't high enough. High seas and breaking waves brought water pouring down the air shafts.

What made it so bad was that the engines controlling the air fans were turned by leather belts. When the water flowed down the shafts, those belts got wet. They stretched. They went slack. The pumps slowed. Less fresh air was pulled in. With so little air, the engines—which needed air—stopped.

The water got even higher.

At the same time, with no fresh air, our lamp flames all but went out.

Even *that* wasn't the worst!

The burning coal in the boilers sucked up most of the good air and gave off bad gases. That poisonous gas filled the engine area. Pretty soon the whole ship was filled with bad air. People got mixed up, hardly knowing where they were or what they were supposed to be doing.

People started passing out.

What happened? Panic! A scramble for the ladder to get to the turret top—just to breathe, just to live.

I myself passed out cold.

CHAPTER TWENTY-THREE

Desperate

WHEN I WOKE, I was on my back, atop the turret, gasping for breath, lashed by hard rain, doused by waves. Someone—I never knew who—had gotten me to safety. I wasn't the only one atop the turret. The whole crew was there! No one was at the wheel.

There we lay, away from the bad gas, but at the maniac mauling of crashing waves and the tossing, turning *Monitor*.

I managed to sit up and look about. No one was talking.

Then Isaac Newton, our chief engineer, plunged below, trying to find a way to put out the boiler fires, start the pumps, and get rid of those gases. He passed out. Paymaster Keeler, struggling to breathe, somehow managed to haul him out to safety.

Inside the *Monitor*, water was still rising.

No one said it, but everyone knew: we were about to sink. Over the roaring wind and crashing waves, I heard Captain Worden and Mr. Greene talk of abandoning the ship. Should they cut the towrope?

Mr. Greene dashed below and came back with a still-lit red lantern. He tried to signal the *Seth Low*. He shouted through the speaking horn, "*Help!*" But the weather was so wild that the *Seth Low* wasn't able to see or hear us. She kept hauling us forward.

I was wet, cold, and scared. Everybody was. There was fear on most faces—including officers. I thought of my ma and Dora. I thought of my pa, too, and wondered how he had died.

When Mr. Newton recovered, he and Mr. Stimers tried to think what to do. First they figured out what had to be done to repair things. Then they sent men down to the engine room. Each was supposed to do just one task, then get back to open air before they passed out.

I volunteered. They told me to go down to the officers' berth and shut any open doors. I was given a soaking-wet cloth to cover my nose and mouth.

I got to my feet, pressed the cloth to my face, then went down the turret ladder one-handed. It was very dim. The water was up to my knees. I saw things floating about—a book, a cup, and a shoe.

The *Monitor* during the storm.

With one hand to a wall to steady myself, I sloshed forward. In the officers' quarters I saw four doors swinging back and forth like dogs' tails. Staggering forward, I tried to shut one of them. The water held it back. Without thinking, I used my second hand to push. My nose cloth dropped away. As I pushed the door, I began to feel groggy. Summoning all my strength, I shoved. The door shut.

Feeling worse and really wobbly, I started to shut a second door. I became dizzy and frightened. Suddenly frantic, I plunged back toward the ladder. Someone rushed past me, going the other direction.

Eventually I reached the turret top—in the end I was hauled up by someone—and knelt down, gasping for air while a wave dashed over me, soaking me anew.

But slowly, with each crew member doing one task at a time, things began to work. First one air pump, then a second, began to slowly work. With the air blowers doing what they were supposed to do, more men could work below. That meant more repairs. Repairs got the pump engines going better and better.

At the same time, the storm began to ease off. Captain Worden was finally able to signal the *Seth Low*. He got her to tow us closer in toward shore, where there would be calmer seas.

By four in the afternoon, things became easier. We

were exhausted, wet, and cold, but the *Monitor* had survived. As best we could, we relaxed, ready for the next night.

Then, about midnight, even as we tried to rest and clean up, the tiller ropes that controlled our steering slipped—they must have gotten wet like those leather engine belts. We couldn't steer the ship.

It was Mr. Stimers who fixed it.

Could we rest? No. Water began pouring in through the anchor well beneath the ship, by way of the hole through which the anchor rope ran—the hawse pipe. It made the most terrifying sound, like the death groans of many men. Really scary. That, too, was repaired. I don't know how.

It wasn't 'til three in the morning that all became truly calm. But though no one slept that night, we were alive—and afloat. The only thing to think about was what was up ahead: the sea monster, the *Merrimac*.

CHAPTER TWENTY-FOUR

We Arrive at Hampton Roads

BY THE DAWN OF MARCH EIGHTH we had unruffled seas. It was warmer, too. But everything was damp and clammy. No one, including me, had really slept during the last two days. I took some time atop the turret, sitting in the sun, breathing in fresh air. As I sat there, I wasn't so sure anymore that I wanted to spend my life at sea.

After Mr. Greene did a general inspection, the crew spent most of their time trying to dry the ship out with rags, mops, and pails. Wasn't easy. Lots of broken crockery, furniture, and junk went into the sea.

Then Captain Worden discovered that during the wildness of the trip, the speaking tube had broken. This was the tube that allowed the captain in the pilothouse and the turret commander to communicate—their sole way of talking to each other. The only ones who would be able to see outside the *Monitor* during a battle were those in the pilothouse. The crew in the turret couldn't see much of anything.

When repairs proved impossible, the captain and Mr. Greene tried to figure out how to proceed. They made some chalk marks on the turret floor so the gun crew would know which side was which, port and starboard. But as they talked, they kept looking at me.

"Master Tom," the captain asked, "is your voice loud?"

I said, "Used to call newspaper headlines."

They didn't say more, not then.

About noon—still under tow and our engines clanking—we passed Cape Charles. We'd finally reached the Chesapeake Bay. When word went out to the crew, everybody got the shivers. We were getting close. The enemy was near.

Then our towrope broke. Captain Worden, fed up, decided that since we were in coastal waters—and everything tranquil—we best not take the time for repairs. So, with black smoke blowing from our stack, we kept on under our own power. The *Seth Low*, like a nervous mother duck, stayed close.

The day became calmer, with a clear blue sky and a few high, white, fluffy clouds. Warm, almost. I began to forget all the terrible things that had happened.

It was near four p.m. when we passed Cape Henry. That put us fifteen miles from Hampton Roads. I was up on the turret with Mr. Greene. As we steamed on, I started hearing something that sounded like thunder. Saw flashes of light, too—like lightning.

"That another storm?" I asked Mr. Green.

He shook his head. "That's cannon."

It wasn't just occasional cannon fire either, but a constant *thud-thud*.

"Heavy guns," said Mr. Greene. The closer we drew in, the more I felt the pressure of the blasts in my ears. I began to see clouds of black and gray smoke. When we passed Fortress Monroe, I saw dark spots in the air.

It was Captain Worden who said, "Bursting shells."

We had reached the war.

From the turret top, Captain Worden and Mr. Greene peered with their telescopes. We passed lots of ships. Many were sail. A few paddle steamers. Most were part of the Union blockade fleet. But one crew member pointed out that there were warships from England and France. "How come they're here?" I asked.

"Bet they're waiting," was the answer. "Waiting to see which side to line up with—depending on the outcome of our battle."

Halfway between Cape Henry and Fortress Monroe, just outside the Roads, a small sailboat nosed out and headed for us. It drew close, then sheered off. A man stood up in its bow. "Jacob Berents, sir," he called. "I'm your pilot through the Roads. Request permission to come aboard, sir."

Captain Worden offered a relaxed salute. "You may come aboard, sir."

The cutter eased along the deck of the *Monitor*.

"Help him, Tom," the captain told me.

I dropped down the ladder and went along the deck. A sailor from the cutter threw me a rope. I held it, drew the cutter in, and Mr. Berents stepped onto the *Monitor*. An elderly, wrinkle-faced man, he looked about the ship, clearly puzzled.

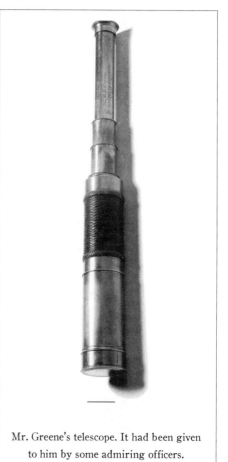

Mr. Greene's telescope. It had been given to him by some admiring officers.

Fortress Monroe, the largest fort in the United States.
Robert E. Lee had been an officer here before the war. After the war
the Confederate president, Jefferson Davis, was in prison here.

"Welcome aboard the *Monitor*, Mr. Berents," the captain called down to him. "We heard cannon fire. What news?"

The man stopped his gaping about. Squinting, he

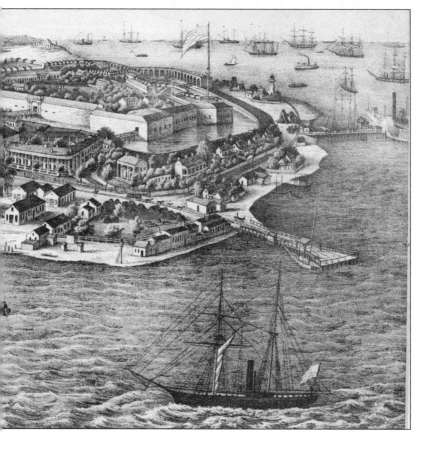

looked up at the captain. "News, sir? Then you don't know?"

"Don't know what?"

He said, "The *Merrimac*'s come out and been on a rampage! We're being slaughtered!"

CHAPTER TWENTY-FIVE

The Pilot's News

"EXACTLY what's happened?" Captain Worden demanded.

"It's the Rebel ironclad, sir," said Mr. Berents. "The *Merrimac*. She's attacked."

"Today?"

"Shortly before noon."

The captain's pale face became red, his fingers agitated. "What does she look like?" he asked.

"Long, low, and huge. Thick with cannons."

"And she's ironclad?"

"Pretty certain, sir. Hard to describe. Never seen her likes before. Terrible strange. All I can tell you is her cannons are enclosed under what looks like an iron roof with sides sloping all around."

"Did she do any damage?"

"*Damage!*" cried Mr. Berents. "God protect you, sir! First, she came out and laid a broadside on the *Congress*. We could see it from the fortress, sir. The *Congress* was so unprepared, she had her laundry drying on the spars. Terrible slaughter."

"Any more?"

"Much more, sir. That *Merrimac* seems to have a ram. She used it on the *Cumberland*, sir. Smashed a hole in her hull big enough to drive a horse and buggy through. Something awful. But she went down with her guns still firing. You can see her top gallants above the water."

"Sank!"

"Yes, sir, and still burning. Then the Rebs went back to the *Congress*. Forced her to fly a white flag."

"And the *Minnesota*, what of her, man?"

"Coming to that. Well, sir, the *Minnesota* tried to run but went aground on a shoal. If ever there was a sitting duck, God mercy her, there she was.

"Sure enough, the *Merrimac* went at her. I'll say this: that ironclad does turn slow. Even so, she would have sunk the *Minnesota* if she hadn't come about and headed back to Norfolk. Don't know why. Maybe because night was coming. Or the tide was turning. Or her ammunition low. Can't rightly say."

"But the *Minnesota* has forty guns!" cried the captain. "Didn't she use them?"

"Use them? They *all* used them. The *Congress* with her fifty. The *Cumberland* with her twenty-four. Blazing away even as they went down. It was something amazing to see."

"And?"

"They might as well have been throwing boiled taters at a rampaging bull for all the damage they done."

The sinking of the *Cumberland* when the *Merrimac* rammed her.
The ram stuck in the *Cumberland* and almost sank the *Merrimac*.
She worked free but lost the ram, which we didn't know.

"Nothing?"

"Nothing anyone could see, sir. Our shot slipped and skittered off that iron beast like skipped stones on a calm pond. Not a scratch! From what I saw, I'd say that ship can't be touched. Like magic. Yes, sir, the whole Blockade Squadron is set to take flight. I never believed I'd see the day."

The captain turned away and stared off into a distance of his own measure. Then I heard him say, "How many killed?"

"They say almost three hundred. Maybe more. Even that's not all, sir. The *Saint Lawrence* grounded herself trying to scoot away. The *Roanoke* daren't draw close. I tell you, Captain, our blockade is all but broke."

"Where did the *Merrimac* go?"

"Back over to her base at Sewell's Point."

"Heaven help us!" said Worden in exasperation. "We've come a day too late!"

"A day too late for what?"

"To fight her."

Mr. Berents looked around as if considering the *Monitor* in a new way. "Fight?" he asked, clearly puzzled. "With what?"

"With this ship, Mr. Berents," cried the angry captain. "This ship!"

Mr. Berents considered a moment before saying, "Do you truly think so, sir?"

"I know so!"

"Hate to tell you, Captain," said Mr. Berents, squinting up. "That *Merrimac*, she's bound to come back tomorrow. She'll want to finish her bloody work. With all respect, sir, I suggest you keep out of her way. I sure don't want no part of her. No, sir, I'll take you up the Roads to anchor. No farther. My advice, sir: head back north."

Captain Worden made no response. What could he say? He led Mr. Berents to the pilothouse. When I got below, members of the crew called out, "Tom! Tom! What news?"

I told them. As my report about the *Merrimac* spread among the crew, the mood turned bleak. And when I told them that the pilot had refused to stay on board, you never saw such dismal faces.

March 8, 1862

THE PHILADELPHIA INQUIRER

HIGHLY IMPORTANT NEWS!

OUR FLEET AT FORTRESS MONROE

ATTACKED

by Rebel Steamers

THE U.S.S. CUMBERLAND

SUNK!

U.S.S. CONGRESS
BURNED

CHAPTER TWENTY-SIX

I See a Sight I Never Wish to See Again

T HE *MONITOR*—piloted by Mr. Berents—entered Hampton Roads close to sundown.

Night proved easy and mild. The moon was in its second quarter, with just enough light to witness what the pilot had told us. It was something awful: the *Cumberland* had sunk, but her flag was still flying from her top mast. The *Congress*, not so much blown apart, but smoldering. Now and again I saw a swirling lick of flame on her spars.

The captain issued orders. Of course, he didn't know when the *Merrimac* might return. Just certain she would. So we prepared ourselves for battle. Smokestack and blower funnels down. Covers screwed over the glass deck windows. Everything movable cleared from the deck and turret. Turret levered up, ready to turn. As much shot and powder in the turret as we could fit. The Stars and Stripes at the stern. Navy jack at the bow.

Then someone discovered that all the water we'd taken in the storm had made things rusty, so everyone set to scraping it off, lubricating whatever needed to move.

Since our Mr. Berents was too fearful to go with us, Captain Worden sent an urgent message to Fortress Monroe for another pilot to guide us through the Roads' shoals. We had to have someone for the next day. It took a long time to get one. But finally, a Mr. Samuel Howard came aboard from the *Amanda*.

Another boat came from the fortress to bring orders. Captain Worden read the message, then called the crew up on the deck.

Looking down from the turret, he said, "Gentlemen, you have already learned of the day's terrible events. I shall not dwell on them. Regardless, we have received our orders. We are ordered to go to the assistance of the *Minnesota*. She is the key, here. We *must* protect her."

No crew member spoke a word.

The captain went on. "I've composed a message to the Secretary of the Navy and asked that it be telegraphed to Washington. I wrote, 'I have the honor to report that I have arrived at anchorage at nine o'clock this evening and am ordered to proceed immediately to the assistance of the *Minnesota* aground near Newport News.'

"Gentlemen, I have every expectation that the *Merrimac* will return and continue her attack. I cannot tell you when she will come, only that she surely will. We shall stay on alert. Gentlemen, we must stop her. And we will. But there will be a battle."

That night, the *Monitor* anchored in water ten fathoms deep, halfway between Fort Monroe and the town of Newport News. We lay aside the *Minnesota*. Compared to us, that *Minnesota* was a mountain. But we were there to protect her.

The captain of the *Minnesota* spoke to Captain Worden. He told Worden that if the *Monitor* failed to save his ship, he would destroy her rather than surrender her to the Rebels.

Everyone knew what that meant. If the *Minnesota* was gone, so was the Union blockade. That made me recall O'Keefe's words: if the blockade failed, the Union cause would be lost.

Most of our crew, worn out from so little sleep and food, stayed below. It was pretty warm down there. Sailors muttered about how many oysters there were below our ship, but how we couldn't get at them. All we had was moldy bread and bad coffee.

Too tense to sleep, I stayed up with the night watch. They filled my head with tales of battles they had fought. The stories, full of screaming cannonballs, splintering wood, and smashed bodies, touched me with dread. I kept thinking about my father. Had he seen such things? Would I ever see Brooklyn again?

When things quieted down, I climbed off the turret and went out to the bow of the ship. I looked about. Over to the north, around Fortress Monroe, I could see lots of campfires burning. Union troops. To the south, at Sewell's Point and Craney Island, just as many flares from Reb troops.

I got goose bumps on my arms when I understood what I was seeing. Thousands of troops—friend and foe alike—would be watching us, looking to see who won.

And I couldn't keep my eyes from the *Congress*. She was still burning. Dreadful to watch. Flames were slowly crawling up her rigging, going ever higher. The burning masts and spars reminded me of a spider's web—threads red hot against the dark night.

Sometime after midnight a series of explosions began. Ever faster, ever louder—powder cases, cannons, and shells exploded. The fire must have reached the *Congress*'s gunpowder stores. With a roar that hurt so much I had to clap my hands over my ears, I saw a sight the likes of which I hope never to see again: a gigantic

The awful end of the *Congress*. At least some of the crew got away.

burst of flame leaped up. It went so high it was like hell was attacking heaven. The night sky was filled with a billion flaming bits. Then, as if the stars themselves had broken loose, the pieces began to drift down. Every time an ember hit the water, it hissed.

The *Congress* breathed flutters of flame like a dying man's last breath. Don't ask me why, but in my head I could see Mr. Quinn grinning at me.

Finally, the dim light of dawn came creeping in from the east. Not so far from where we lay, I could see the all-but-sunken *Cumberland*. Her Stars and Stripes were still flying at her peak.

I wondered, Is that a sign of bravery or despair?

We were about to find out.

CHAPTER TWENTY-SEVEN

The Morning of March 9, 1862

W E TOOK UP ANCHORAGE behind the *Minnesota*. Just sat there waiting for the *Merrimac* to steam back into the Roads from the Elizabeth River, where she'd gone for the night. Like a sea monster in its lair, I thought. When she came up, she wouldn't see us. Not at first.

Did I want her to return?

I was scared. I mean, I had no experience of deadly battle. Was the *Monitor* going to be *Ericsson's Folly*? Or was she going to teach them Rebs a lesson? I knew the *Monitor*. I knew what was strong about her—how different she was, her iron-plated turret, her two great guns, her crew.

But we *had* almost sunk. We had almost abandoned her. And I could think of four weak points.

What would happen if a shot dropped straight down

on our deck? No eight inches of iron-plate protection there—as the turret had—just *two* inches.

What would happen when an iron shot smashed the turret? Would the rivets and bolts hold?

What if a shot struck dead-on where the deck folded over the hull? Were we weak there?

What about that *Merrimac's* ram, which the pilot had told us about? It had sunk the *Cumberland*, hadn't it? What if she used it against us?

I kept telling myself, *Nothing bad's gonna happen.* If I thought that once, I thought it a million times. But I couldn't get my pa, and what had happened to him, out of my head.

Then night drifted off, and the new day—Sunday, March ninth—seeped in, bringing a low fog over Hampton Roads. Vapor rising up from the bay waters made it look as if the water was smoldering.

Tension on board was high. It wasn't just not knowing what was about to happen. It was wanting things to *start* happening.

I helped pass out coffee and bread.

Not long after, Worden had us piped to quarters. That's sailor talk for "get ready for battle."

The captain took his place—wearing his sword!—in the pilothouse. He stood there with the pilot, Mr. Howard, and the helmsman, Mr. Williams. Mr. Greene was in command in the turret. Mr. Stodder was at the turret controls. Mr. Stimers was there too, overseeing. The gun crew, our sixteen strongest men, were stripped to their waists. Mr. Stocking and Mr. Lochrave were the gun captains, each one in charge of a single cannon.

Isaac Newton was in the engine room below. He had coal heavers, firemen, oilers, and a water tender under his command. Boilers needed constant minding, and there were lots of gauges to check, oil cups to keep full.

And, oh! I was sure wishing I hadn't seen the surgeon lay out his ghastly tools—saws, pincers, knives—on the officers' table.

Someone was in charge of the powder magazine on the berth deck. A crew was ready to hoist shot and powder when needed.

Where was I?

Remember me saying that the speaking tube—the way the captain and the men in the turret talked to each other—had broken during the storm?

The captain called me to him.

"Mr. Carroll," he said to me, first time he'd used that *Mr*. "It'll have to be you who carries my orders to the turret. I'll give a command. You dash aft and shout it up. Can you do it? It's a crucial task."

"Yes, sir," I said, my heart thudding.

He handed me his speaking trumpet. "This will

make your voice even louder. Now, get on up to the turret," he said. "The *Minnesota* will tell us when the *Merrimac* appears."

"Yes, sir," I said, and ran to do as ordered.

Fact is, I felt a whole lot better. I'd been worried that I'd have *nothing* to do. Now I had something—something big. I was glad I'd shouted out newspaper headlines.

Since we were behind the *Minnesota*, the *Merrimac* couldn't see us. Of course, we couldn't see her either. Even if she had seen us, not sure it would have mattered. She'd be coming no matter what.

I stood on the turret, so tired I think I actually dozed off. Suddenly I heard, "The *Merrimac*! She's coming!"

Between seven and seven thirty that morning, the *Merrimac* had poked her snout out of the Elizabeth River. As bold as marching music, she steamed into the Roads.

One of the *Minnesota*'s officers was shouting down to me. "The *Merrimac*! She's coming right at us!"

I fairly dove into the turret, making sure I closed the hatch behind me. "She's coming!" I shouted over and over again as I ran down the galleyway to the pilot-house.

"Up anchor!" the captain cried.

Next moment, I heard the anchor crank turn.

I heard the captain say, "Very well, Mr. Williams, come 'round the *Minnesota* and then proceed straight ahead, right at the *Merrimac*. Mr. Carroll, tell the turret what we are about."

I tore down the galleyway—it was about seventy-five feet back to the turret—yelling through the speaking horn, "We're going to meet her! We're going to meet her!"

It was about eight thirty in the morning. The only two sounds I could hear were the *clank-clank* of the engine and my heart hammering.

According to the captain, the morning's fog—just like a theater curtain—had lifted. The battle was about to begin.

CHAPTER TWENTY-EIGHT

The Battle Starts

I RACED BACK TO the pilothouse and looked up. Captain Worden and the pilot had their faces pressed to the viewing slots so they could see what was happening. Mr. Williams was at the wheel, awaiting orders. To my surprise, the captain climbed down to where I was. "Tom, come along," he said to me, sounding fairly calm.

He went down along the galley and up into the turret. "Mr. Greene," he called. "You and I need to take a look."

As we climbed up, we were just coming around the *Minnesota*. From atop the turret, Captain Worden could study the *Merrimac*, and not just through the slots in the pilothouse.

It was a frightening sight. To my eyes, the *Merrimac*, heading right toward us, seemed *gigantic*, a monster

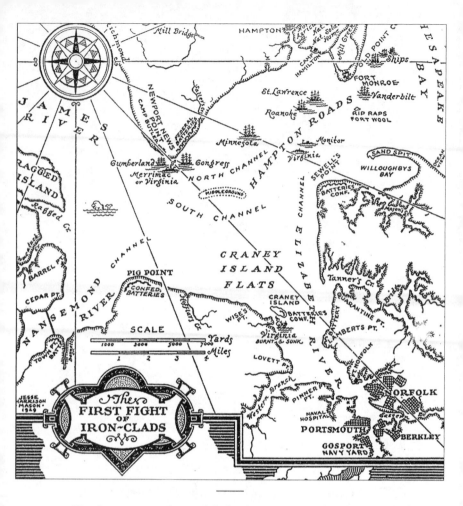

Here is a pretty good map of the battle area. Just south of Newport News
you can see where the *Congress* and the *Cumberland* were attacked.
Right over where it reads "Hampton Roads" is the *Minnesota*.
Right under is where our two ships fought. Confederate troops were
looking on from Sewell's Point. Union forces looked on from Fort Monroe.

with thick black smoke streaming behind her like a galloping horse's mane.

1 6 8

Here's some of what I learned about the *Merrimac*, then and later:

The Reb ironclad was about a hundred feet longer than the *Monitor*. She looked even bigger. She had a ram at her bow. She was wider than we were and had a draft (depth) of twenty-two feet. The *Monitor* had eleven. She had a crew of three hundred and fifty. We had fifty-eight.

The *Merrimac* had this sloping iron roof that ran along pretty much the whole ship. Poking out of each sloping side were three cannons, nine-inch Dahlgrens, plus two Brooke rifled cannons. Plus two more Brooke rifled cannons at bow and stern. She could load and fire every five minutes.

The *Monitor* carried *two* eleven-inch Dahlgren cannons. It took us between seven or eight minutes to shoot them off.

They had even coated the *Merrimac*'s roof with pig fat so enemy shots would skid off. No fat on us.

Two wooden gunboat steamers came along with her.

We were alone.

In other words, the *Merrimac* was bigger, had a larger crew, had more guns than the *Monitor*, and could shoot faster.

That was the sea monster we were going to fight.

I couldn't imagine then what the *Merrimac* thought

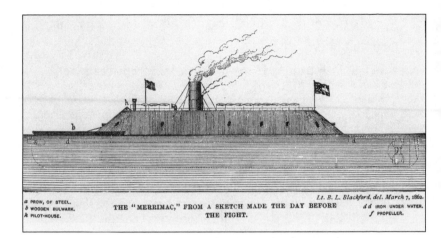

a PROW, OF STEEL.
b WOODEN BULWARK.
h PILOT-HOUSE.

THE "MERRIMAC," FROM A SKETCH MADE THE DAY BEFORE
THE FIGHT.

Lt. B. L. Blackford, del. March 7, 1862.
d d IRON UNDER WATER.
f PROPELLER.

of us. Later we got word that they didn't know *what* we were. She certainly didn't understand that our turret held cannons or could turn. How could she? No other turret existed. And I never had said anything to Mr. Quinn. In fact, at first they thought we were some kind of *water* tanker. "Tin can on a shingle," one of the *Merrimac* crew called to us.

The point is, the *Merrimac* didn't act as if she had a bug's breath of worry about us, that we could do her the slightest harm. She steamed steady on toward the *Minnesota,* coming to finish her off.

"What do you think, Mr. Carroll?" the captain asked me.

I said, "We're like a city rat attacking a Southern alligator."

Mr. Greene and the captain laughed. I guess I understood then why I was there: they liked a youngster aboard, someone who saw things different than they did.

The next moment, the *Merrimac* opened fire. Wasn't at us, but one of her shells howled over our heads. It struck the side of the *Minnesota* with a *crash* and burst of wood splinters. Scared the breath out of me.

The captain, nothing but calm, said, "Gentlemen, we'd best go below."

Back in the pilothouse, the captain said to Mr. Howard, "I want to engage that ship as far from the *Minnesota* as possible. Make sure we are always between the *Merrimac* and the *Minnesota*. The only way she can get to her must be *over* us."

"Yes, sir," said Mr. Howard, and he gave orders to the helmsmen.

The captain turned to me: "Tell Mr. Green what we are doing."

I bolted off again, racing back and forth between the turret and the pilothouse.

Mr. Greene to me: "Mr. Carroll, ask the captain if I should fire."

He had to ask because the turret crew had no idea where the *Merrimac* was. The gun ports were covered by very heavy iron shutters. Those shutters were designed to keep enemy cannon fire out, but it also meant the crew couldn't see much of anything.

I dashed back.

The captain to me: "Tell Mr. Greene not to fire until I give word, then to be cool and deliberate, take sure aim, and not waste a shot."

Mr. Greene to me: "Tell the captain we are standing ready."

Me to Captain Worden: "He's ready!"

He to me: "Double check."

I shouted up from beneath the turret: "Mr. Greene, sir? Are you truly ready?"

"Ready and waiting," came the reply. "Ask if I shall fire!" One of the cannons, loaded with charge and shot, had been run out.

Captain to me: "Tell Mr. Greene that I am going to bring her close alongside our starboard beam."

I tore back. Mr. Greene was leaning over the cannon, trying to see the *Merrimac*.

"Shall I begin?"

I ran back to the captain.

The *Monitor* had pulled herself alongside the *Merrimac*, and then stopped. We were only yards apart!

"Commence firing!" the captain shouted, and I ran down the galley and screamed the order. Next moment, Mr. Greene stepped back and yanked the lanyard on his cannon. It roared. That spent cannon was hauled back. The second cannon was run up and fired.

I tell you, when our cannons fired, no noise had ever been so loud. I did not just hear it in my ears, I *felt* it in my eyes, mouth, my whole body. Many a nose bled, and all eyes were teary from the explosions. Smoke was everywhere.

As soon as they fired, the turret began to rotate.

The fifteen-pound bags of gunpowder were easy enough to carry and plump into the cannons. But to carry each cannonball—a hundred and sixty-five pounds!—required two men, the strongest backs and hands, plus a stretcher, slings, and pulleys.

After our first shots went off, the *Merrimac* could have no doubt as to why we were there. And no doubt as to her response. I felt a terrible suspense. What would happen to us when she fired and we were struck?

We found out soon enough.

It took just moments for the *Merrimac* to heave a broadside at us with four of her cannons.

First to come was the shrill, screaming shriek of the incoming shots. Then came an ear-breaking *clang!* as a metal shell struck the turret and exploded. The concussion was enormous. The whole turret shook. I felt it all over my body.

But when that shell struck us, the result was . . .

nothing! Nothing but noise and shaking.

Let me tell you, every crew member's face sparked to life. And those faces said, *Nothing happened! We won't be harmed! The iron has protected us!*

Captain Ericsson had been right.

Maybe so, but Mr. Greene still had doubts. After the first exchange of broadsides—while our cannons were being reloaded—he scrambled out of the turret. As he told us later, he laid out flat and peered down, wanting to see what the *Merrimac's* shot had done to us. All

A battle scene showing the *Monitor* trying to shield the U.S. Navy
flagship *Minnesota* from the *Merrimac*.

the time he was in danger of losing his life, since *Merrimac* sharpshooters were aiming at him. But the *Monitor* was constantly moving, circling the *Merrimac*, and he hadn't been hit. Brave man.

He scurried back to report we'd suffered no harm.

The turret crew cheered!

Meanwhile, the turret had swung away. We fired another round. Another. And another.

It was hard to see. It was hard to breathe. Gases drifted up from the fire room and mixed with the gun smoke. More smoke and heat eddied from our oil lamps. All mixed with the stench of the nineteen-man crew sweating in that small turret, working in a hot frenzy. Sweat dripped down through the hatches into the berth deck

In the turret, the smoke was so thick, noise so loud, shocks huge and constant, it was as if we were in a world of dark clouds, a place where gods make terrible iron thunder and blinding lightning bolts. Why, even the gun crew, covered with black powder, were like creatures from another world. In the midst of it all, orders were constantly being shouted. Cannons boomed. Chaos!

The battle didn't stop. Shot after shot was exchanged.

The men in the engine room below, under the steady commands of Mr. Newton, were heaving coal into the fireboxes, keeping the boiler steam at bursting levels for the engines that moved the turret and the propeller. Same time, they were checking engines, gauges, pressure, oil.

Mr. Greene would cry down to me, "How does the *Merrimac* bear?"

I raced his question to the captain.

His reply: "On the starboard beam." Or: "On the port quarter."

But the chalk marks on the turret floor were quickly gone.

The *Merrimac* had armed herself to go after wooden ships, so she was firing explosive shells. We were shooting solid shot. This gave us a great advantage, although Mr. Greene expressed the wish that he'd been permitted to use heavier powder charges so as to throw his shots with greater force.

All during this time, I kept galloping back and forth between the pilothouse and turning turret.

Pretty soon a whole new trouble was discovered. While the turret turned easily, once it halted it took precious moments to get it moving again. And once moving, it was hard to stop. The lifting and lowering of the gun port shutters took too much time and energy. So Mr. Greene ordered them left open. But to protect the crew while they reloaded, he kept the turret constantly moving, slow and stately. That way the *Merrimac* only saw the solid turret walls, save when our cannons spoke.

While the gun crews worked frantically to clean cannons and reload, Mr. Greene leaned over the gun barrels, sighting. Soon as the turret spun so that the *Merrimac* hove into view, he yanked the lanyards and fired anew.

It was the best that we could do. It worked . . . mainly. Yes, we often missed the *Merrimac*, but again and again we struck her dead-on. But though she kept losing her flag (and replacing it), and despite our close range barrage, she didn't retreat.

Nor did we. And with neither ironclad retreating, the battle thundered on.

March 10, 1862

The New York Times

ATTACK
upon our Blockading Vessels
by the Rebel Steamer
MERRIMAC

OPPORTUNE ARRIVAL
OF THE
IRON CLAD
ERICSSON BATTERY MONITOR

DESPERATE
NAVAL ENGAGEMENT AT
HAMPTON ROADS

CHAPTER TWENTY-NINE

The Battle Continues

THE *MERRIMAC* tried again and again to hit the *Minnesota*. But Captain Worden put the *Monitor* in front of the stranded flagship. Between the two ironclads, the *Monitor* could move better, faster. And because our hull wasn't very deep compared to hers, and Hampton Roads had a maze of shoals, we could go where the *Merrimac* could not. Being longer meant the *Merrimac* took more time to turn about, too.

So Captain Worden had us moving constantly, circling, trying to find the *Merrimac*'s weakness—*if* there was one.

Fact is, the two ships were nearly touching but still hurling broadside for broadside at each other.

Smoke enveloped us both, and we were in the center of the storm.

Then too, with Mr. Greene having made the decision to keep the gun ports open, that meant when we did swing around, marksmen on the *Merrimac* tried to shoot through our gun ports. Fortunately, that didn't work.

Another thing: because from time to time the *Minnesota* tried to shoot the enemy, sometimes she hit us!

No one was hurt on our ship. The only thing close was when Mr. Stoddard, of the gun crew, was leaning against the turret wall when a shot from the *Merrimac* slammed into us. Stoddard hadn't been hit, but the force of that blow striking the iron plates stunned him with a concussion. Had to go below to be attended by the surgeon.

At one point, the captain, with his eyes as always pressed to the viewing slots, called to me: "Mr. Carroll," he said, "tell Mr. Greene I think they are preparing a boarding party. He should load with canister shot!"

A whole new danger. Now I knew why the captain wore a sword! Wished I had one.

As I raced to deliver the message, I wondered what I would—or could—do. *A boarding party!* It was nothing I'd ever even considered. I delivered the message to Mr. Greene, but didn't run back, waiting to see what would happen. Five of the gun crew grabbed rifles and stood under the ladder that went to the top of the turret. At the same time, Mr. Greene yanked the lanyards and fired off two more shots.

As the smoke cleared, I heard him say, "They'll never board now." I couldn't see what he'd done.

The battled raged on.

From time to time the turret ran out of cannon shot. When I passed on the word to Captain Worden, he ordered the *Monitor* to withdraw for a few moments to a shallow place where the *Merrimac* could not follow. Then we swung our turret about to align the scuttle hole with the hole above the powder storage area. Heavy shot was hoisted up as fast as possible.

During one such time, the *Merrimac* tried to slip past us, but only succeeded in running aground. She couldn't move.

"Bring us around to her stern," Captain Worden commanded. I could tell he was excited.

To me he said, "Tell Mr. Greene what's happened. I intend to cross that ship. When I do, he must fire!"

I tore down to deliver the message, and then raced back. I found the captain, face pressed against the viewing slots, saying, "She's trying to pull off!"

Even as he spoke, we unloaded shots at her stern.

"She's broken free!" called our pilot.

In fact, the *Merrimac* had not only broken free but

This picture shows just how close our two ships came!

was coming around and heading right at us!

"Look out, now!" cried the captain. "She has a ram. She's trying to hit us. Mr. Carroll, tell Mr. Greene to give them both guns to keep her off!"

I was running back with the message when I felt a massive jolt, enough to throw me off my feet. The *Merrimac* had struck us a glancing blow on the starboard quarter. Same moment we sent off another shot. Even so, the blow from the *Merrimac* caused the *Monitor* to lurch about. Our engines *clanked* the more. But then our motion evened out. We had not been harmed.

The battle continued as fiercely as before.

Close to noon, needing to replenish our ammunition

and shot supplies, we retired to shallower water. Good thing, too: everyone was exhausted.

Then Captain Worden announced that the *Merrimac* was making another attack on the *Minnesota*. He ordered us back into the fray. He shouted down to me: "Tell Mr. Greene I am going to try to ram her. Tell Mr. Newton I want top speed!"

I raced toward the engine room, shouting orders. The coal heavers glistened with sweat and black coal dust. The *Monitor* swung about.

I ran back just in time to hear the captain shout, "Just missed her!"

The smoke and cannon noise were incredible!

I stood below the pilothouse, staring up, waiting for orders. That's when I saw a flash of light followed by a loud *crack!* A cloud of smoke poured through the pilot box.

"My eyes!" the captain cried. He staggered back, hands clapped to his face. Blood was streaming down his cheeks. "Sheer off! Sheer off!"

An exploding shell had struck the pilothouse.

I stood there, horrified. Then, recollecting myself, I tore down the galley, crying for the surgeon. "Captain's been wounded! Captain's been wounded!"

As the surgeon rushed past me, I shouted up to the turret, "Mr. Greene! Mr. Greene! Captain's been wounded."

In moments we were beneath the pilothouse, the captain on the floor, attended by the doctor. Mr. Greene knelt by the wounded captain.

"Mr. Greene," I heard the captain say. "I'm blind! Take command. Save the *Minnesota* if you can."

Mr. Greene shouted up to the helmsman, "Back us off!"

Then the doctor, Mr. Greene, and I carried the captain to his rooms. Laid him on his bed. The doctor began to work on Captain Worden's eyes. We stood there helplessly.

As if suddenly realizing the ship was under his command, Mr. Greene raced back to the pilothouse, and

Viewing the battle from near Newport News.
It was amazing how many people watched the battle from both shores.

I followed. By the time we got there, perhaps twenty minutes had gone by.

He poked his head up into the pilothouse to survey the damage. It had been just one shot, a shell that had exploded right up against the bars. One iron brace had been shattered. That was the explosion that had wounded the captain.

Mr. Greene peered through the pilothouse slots to see what had occurred. "By God!" he cried. "The *Merrimac's* retreating."

"Tom," he shouted at me. "Get the other officers here!"

No doubt: the *Merrimac* was leaving the Roads.

Once the officers had assembled, they had a quick council. Greene laid out the question: should they go after the *Merrimac* or follow Captain Worden's last order, to protect the *Minnesota*?

In the end, Mr. Greene choose to follow the captain's orders. So the *Monitor* returned to the side of the *Minnesota*.

Suddenly the battle was over.

March 11, 1862

THE NEW YORK HERALD

THE
GREAT NAVAL
CONFLICT!

The Desperate Struggles of the
Iron Clad Gunboats

TRIUMPH

OF THE ERICSSON BATTERY MONITOR

Statement of the
Pilot of the Cumberland

THE SLOOP OF WAR
WENT DOWN WITH HER COLORS FLYING

TWO HUNDRED LIVES
PROBABLY LOST

Skill and Bravery of
the Officers of the Monitor

THRILLING SCENES AND
INCIDENTS

CHAPTER THIRTY

Who Won?

WE'D BEEN FIGHTING for just about four hours. When we saw the *Merrimac* going away, since most of the crew had been in the hot ship for twelve hours, we raced up to the turret and deck top for fresh air. The *Merrimac* was surely heading back to the Elizabeth River. Far as we could tell, she'd just given up.

I counted some twenty-two dents, mostly in the turret, but not one crack in our iron plating.

A grinning Mr. Geer, who'd been shoveling coal in the engine room, said it best: "I guess they were only flinging spitballs at us."

Seeing the *Merrimac* retreat, knowing that the *Minnesota* was safe, the *Monitor* pulled toward the town of Newport News. As we nosed toward town, folk and soldiers cheered and hurrahed. It felt like the whole world had come out to see us. Pretty soon our deck was crowded with generals and officers congratulating us on our victory, treating us like heroes.

I guess we were.

For dinner I helped serve beefsteak and peas. In the midst of the dinner, a Mr. Gustavus Fox, Assistant Secretary of the Navy, boarded us. Seeing us eating so calmly, he said, "Well, gentlemen, you don't look as though you were just through one of the greatest naval conflicts on record."

Now, the Rebs didn't see it that way. When we pulled back during Captain Worden's injury, they decided it was *us* who'd given up. Claimed *they* had won. No doubt, before we got into the Roads, the *Merrimac* did awful damage to the Federal squadron. Sunk two major Union ships. Seriously damaged another.

They had reason to think they'd won.

But looking back, I'd have to see it another way.

First off, the *Merrimac* had retreated with lots of damage to her iron plating. She was leaking so badly, it took six weeks to repair her.

But the main thing was this: the *Monitor* kept the *Merrimac* from destroying the Union's naval blockade.

Later on, some folks said that what we did in Hampton Roads was more important for the Union cause than the Battle of Gettysburg. From that came the claim that the *Monitor*'s action had doomed the Confederacy. For sure, the *Merrimac* never fought again. Later on, in May, to keep her from falling into Union hands, the Rebs destroyed her.

Captain Worden? In the end he wasn't blinded. He did stay pale in the face with a faint tattoo of powder burn, but he continued to serve on other *Monitor*s and had himself a fine naval career.

What happened to the *Monitor*? She saw very little real action, except we were ordered up the James River and tried to dislodge a rebel battery, but that didn't amount to much. The government in Washington wanted to keep her intact—a symbol of a great victory.

For much of the year, she saw only a little active duty on the James River, but mostly remained where she was, at anchor. But finally on Christmas Day, 1862, we were sent south, ready for major action.

Lord help us! On December thirtieth, the *Monitor* was caught in another big storm. This time in the early morning hours of New Year's Eve, the ship sank to the bottom of the sea. Sixteen men were lost—twelve sailors plus four officers. I was lucky to get off alive.

The *Monitor* had not lived a full year.

What about me? I stayed with the navy, fought on other

The Rebs destroyed the *Merrimac* to keep her out of Union hands.

ironclads. It wasn't the same. When the war was over I went back to Brooklyn. Ma was doing fine. Dora struggled on. I became a carpenter. But I have to admit, there wasn't any greater moment in my life than when I served as one of—it's what we all called ourselves—the *Monitor* boys.

After the battle, the London *Times* wrote: "Whereas England had available for immediate purposes one hundred and forty-nine first-class war ships . . . There is not now a ship in the English navy apart from . . . two ironclads that it would not be madness to trust in an engagement with that little *Monitor*."

Navies 'round the world would never be the same again.

Now one more thing: there's this famous writer, Nathaniel Hawthorne, and when writing about the *Monitor* he said, "How can an admiral condescend to go to sea in an iron pot? All the pomp and splendor of naval warfare are gone by."

I'm here to tell you that Mr. Hawthorne was dead wrong. I know. I was there. I saw it all.

ANCHORAGE: A place where ships anchor

BALLOON SPOTTERS: It was during the Civil War that military observers were first carried aloft in baskets tethered to balloons so as to observe what was happening on the ground.

BATTERY: Military term for cannons

BLOCKADE: A military tactic by which one side tries to prevent the enemy from moving troops or supplies

BOW: The front of a boat

BREECH: The back end of the muzzle on a firearm, where the explosive charge is packed and fired

BRIG: A room used as a jail on a boat. On the *Monitor*, the anchor room was the brig.

CAPSTAN: The wheel on which an anchor cable is wound

CIVIL WAR, 1861–1865: This is a term that came to be used after the war. During the war, the South spoke of it as the War Between the States. The North spoke of the War of the Rebellion.

COME ABOUT: The nautical term for turning around

COPPERHEAD: A person in the Northern states whose sympathies lay with the Confederacy during the war. The term came from antiwar Democrats who wore the copper penny that bore the head of "Lady Liberty" as a badge of opposition to the war. In turn, Union supporters referred to them as vicious snakes.

CREW: The total number of active men on a ship. On the *Monitor*, the crew were quite young, and came from many different places. Pictures reveal that there were also African Americans on the crew.

CUTTER: A sailing boat with one mast

DAHLGREN CANNONS: Invented by John Dahlgren. Dahlgren was in charge of the navy's guns. The Dahlgren cannons were bulbous at the breech end, which allowed for a larger explosive charge. That meant heavier shot could be fired greater distances.

DRAFT: The depth of a ship's hull below the waterline; also, the minimum depth of water a ship needs to float.

FATHOM: The nautical term for measuring water depth. A fathom is six feet. Six fathoms, then, would be thirty-six feet.

FEDS: Federal forces of the United States of America

FLAGSHIP: The primary ship among a fleet of ships. Usually it is the ship from which the admiral of a fleet commands.

FLOATING BATTERY: A raft with cannons on it

GUNBOAT: An armed ship of modest size

GUNPOWDER: When used with cannons, gunpowder was put in pre-weighted cloth bags for ease of loading.

HELMSMAN: The member of the crew who turned—under the captain's orders—the steering wheel

JEFFERSON DAVIS: The first and only president of the Confederate States of America. He had been a former U.S. senator. When the war ended, he was captured and imprisoned at Fort Monroe. He was later released, and no charges were ever brought against him.

KNOT: A nautical term measuring speed. A knot is one nautical mile per hour.

MAGAZINE: The storage place for gunpowder

MERRIMAC: When the Confederates rebuilt the *Merrimac* into an ironclad, they renamed her the *Virginia*. That said, very few in the North referred to her by any name other than the *Merrimac*. In the South, even at the time, the name *Merrimac* was used more often than not.

MONITOR: The name was chosen by John Ericsson, with

the notion that he would teach the Rebels a lesson.

MUTINY: A rebellion on a ship, during which the crew takes control from the officers

NAVY JACK: A jack is a flag. The navy jack is the official navy flag.

ON STATION: The location and task assigned to a navy ship

PADDLE WHEELERS: Most ships were driven by sails. A steam-driven ship, such as the *Merrimac*, had propellers. Paddle wheelers were steamships with large paddle wheels on both sides of the ship. The *Seth Low* is a good example of a paddle wheeler.

PILOT: In coastal waters, bays, and harbors, where waters could be shallow and deep channels hard to locate, it was common to take on a pilot who knew the waters well, and thus could navigate safely.

PORT: The left side of a ship, looking forward

RAM: One of the unusual things about the *Merrimac* was its ram. This was a cast-iron spike set in its bow, designed to pierce the hull of a ship. That is what sank the *Cumberland*. However, unknown to the Union navy, the ram of the *Merrimac* broke off during that engagement. The ram is believed to still be lying under the waters of Hampton Roads.

RUN UP: To roll a cannon forward so that it is ready to fire

SCREW PROPELLER: The kind of propeller that drives

virtually all ships today—from outboard motors to battle-ships. The screw propeller was invented by John Ericsson.

SERVANTS: In 1862, it was common for navy officers to have their own servants. The servants were not considered part of the crew.

SHOAL: A shallow section of water

STARBOARD: The right side of a ship, looking forward

STERN: The rear of the boat

THE UNION: The United States of America

USS: United States Ship

WATCH: Navy crews were divided into watches, which meant that while some slept or were off duty, others worked.

Iron Thunder is a work of fiction based on a real historical event. My intent was to bring that moment to life for my readers.

The saga of the *Monitor* and its epic battle with the Confederate *Merrimac* was witnessed by thousands. Not surprisingly, many—including those directly engaged—wrote about what happened. But there is an old saying: *The more who witness a fact—the less certain that fact becomes.*

To think like a historian, one must be a detective. To be a good detective, one must think like a novelist. To be a good novelist, one must, as writer Paula Fox once observed, "Imagine the truth."

I have told this story from the point of view of a boy on the *Monitor*. There really was a first class boy named Thomas Carroll on the ship, though somewhat older than the Tom depicted here. In fact, he was born in Ireland. That said, most of what my character does is imagined. In that sense, Tom is a composite of many of the people who were on the ship. For instance, I've radically reduced the role Paymaster Keeler had during the battle itself, and put Tom in his place. Not having a record of Captain Worden's appeal to the sailors to volunteer, I tried to imagine his words.

To write this book, I consulted many biographical records, newspaper accounts, and histories, as well as original letters, logs, telegraph messages, memoirs, and reports from people who were either on board the *Monitor* or witnessed what happened. I have used these records to describe what happened and to put words into the mouth of Tom and others. That said, many of the exchanges have been taken right from memoirs or the contemporaneous letters.

It should be stated that some of the facts—even those put forward by witnesses—can and should be disputed. Those upon the *Merrimac* thought they had defeated the *Monitor*. It may be considered a cliché, but there is truth to the notion that victors write the histories, and there can be no question that the forces of the United States defeated the Confederacy.

One of the most interesting aspects of the real story of the *Monitor* is that many of those who were engaged knew they were making history. Not unlike the men who first stepped upon the moon, those on the *Monitor* knew that what they were doing was momentous.

Again, my intent here was to give real history real life. The story of the *Monitor* is extraordinary. I can only hope I have served her well.

In 1973, the wreckage of the *Monitor* was located at the bottom of the sea. Since that time, large parts of it—the turret, its cannons, and engines, plus a vast array of artifacts—have been recovered. They were brought to the Mariners' Museum in

The recovery of the Monitor's turret.

Newport News, Virginia. Here, the USS *Monitor* Center—in partnership with the National Oceanic & Atmospheric Administration—was established, and a new museum for the public display of everything about the *Monitor*, both large and small—from the turret itself to boots and a butter dish—was created.

The museum, however, is more than just a display of objects. Here, one can view a full-size replica of the ship, walk through a reconstruction of the officers' quarters, move through a simulation of the battle itself, and much, much more. This is museum creation at its most modern, accessible, and exciting.

For a great deal of information about the museum, and the *Monitor*, go to www.monitorcenter.org.

BIBLIOGRAPHY

Davis, William C. *Duel Between the First Ironclads*. Baton Rouge: Louisiana State University Press, 1975.

DeKay, James Tertius. *Monitor: The Story of the Legendary Civil War Ironclad and the Man Whose Invention Changed the Course of History*. New York: Walker & Company, 1997.

Donovan, Frank Robert. *Ironclads of the Civil War*. New York: American Heritage Publishing Co., 1964.

Geer, George S. *The Monitor Chronicles. One Sailor's Account*. New York: Simon & Schuster and the Mariners' Museum, 2000.

Keeler, William Frederick. *Aboard the USS Monitor: 1862; The Letters of Acting Paymaster William Frederick Keeler, to His Wife, Anna*. Annapolis, MD: U.S. Naval Institute Press, 1964.

Konstam, Angus. *Duel of the Ironclads: USS Monitor and CSS Virginia at Hampton Roads, 1862*. Nothhants, UK: Osprey, 2003.

Nelson, James L. *Reign of Iron: The Story of the First Battling Ironclads, the Monitor and the Merrimac*. New York: William Morrow, 2004.

Worden, John Lorimer, D. G. Greene, H. A. Ramsay, and E. W. Watson. *The Monitor and the Merrimac: Both Sides of the Story Told by Lieut. J. L. Worden*. New York: Harper and Brothers, 1912.

ACKNOWLEDGMENTS

This book could not have been written without the existence of The Mariners' Museum and Library and its endlessly supportive staff. They provided materials, suggestions, guidance, and corrections when necessary. Particular thanks go to Anna Holloway, Claudia Jew, Lester Weber, and Cathy Williamson. Deep-felt thanks to all.

AVI has written more than sixty books, several of which have garnered prestigious awards, including the Newbery Award and two Newbery Honors. His titles with Hyperion include *Crispin: The Cross of Lead*; *Crispin: At the Edge of the World*; and *The Book Without Words*. He lives with his family in Colorado.